NEW YORK REVIEW BOOKS
CLASSICS

ARIANE

CLAUDE ANET was the pen name of Jean Schopfer (1868–1931), who was born in Morges, Switzerland, to a French Swiss father and an English mother. After studying philosophy, art, and literature at the École du Louvre and the Sorbonne, he became a competitive tennis player, winning the 1892 French Open. In the late 1890s, following a brief stint in business, Schopfer began to publish as Claude Anet (after the romantic rival of Jean-Jacques Rousseau). Art and travel, two of his passions, were the subjects of Anet's early books, including *The Roses of Isfahan: Persia in a Motor Car, by way of Russia and the Caucasus* (1906). Finding himself in Russia at the outbreak of World War I, he fell into the role of war correspondent for a French newspaper. But when he changed his visa to read "civil war correspondent" after the Revolution of 1917, the Bolshevists were not amused, and he was imprisoned. He escaped through Finland and made his way back to Paris, where he soon began to compose what would become his most popular novel, *Ariane, A Russian Girl* (1920; the source of Billy Wilder's 1957 film *Love in the Afternoon*). An avid swimmer, cyclist, golfer, and croquet player, Schopfer also collected art and ran a gallery specializing in Persian miniatures. His last novel, *Mayerling*, was published in 1930, shortly before his death from sepsis at his home on the rue du Bac in Paris.

MITCHELL ABIDOR is a historian and translator of French, Spanish, Italian, Portuguese, and Esperanto. Among the books he has translated and edited are an anthology of Victor Serge's anarchist writings, *Anarchists Never Surrender*; Jean Jaurès's *Socialist History of the French Revolution*; and *May Made Me: An Oral History of the 1968 Uprising in France*. His translation of Serge's *Notebooks: 1936–1937* is published by NYRB Classics. He was born in Brooklyn, New York, where he still lives.

ARIANE

A Russian Girl

CLAUDE ANET

Translated from the French by

MITCHELL ABIDOR

NEW YORK REVIEW BOOKS

New York

THIS IS A NEW YORK REVIEW BOOK
PUBLISHED BY THE NEW YORK REVIEW OF BOOKS
207 East 32nd Street, New York, NY 10016
www.nyrb.com

First published as a New York Review Books Classic in 2023.

Library of Congress Cataloging-in-Publication Data
Names: Anet, Claude, 1868–1931, author. | Abidor, Mitchell, translator.
Title: Ariane, a Russian girl / by Claude Anet; translated by Mitchell Abidor.
Other titles: Ariane, jeune fille russe. English
Description: New York: New York Review Books, [2022] | Series: New York
  Review Books classics
Identifiers: LCCN 2022027631 (print) | LCCN 2022027632 (ebook) |
  ISBN 9781681377100 (paperback) | ISBN 9781681377117 (ebook)
Subjects: LCGFT: Novels.
Classification: LCC PQ2637.C63 A813 2022 (print) | LCC PQ2637.C63 (ebook) |
  DDC 843/.912—dc23/eng/20220705
LC record available at https://lccn.loc.gov/2022027631
LC ebook record available at https://lccn.loc.gov/2022027632

ISBN 978-1-68137-710-0
Available as an electronic book; ISBN 978-1-68137-711-7

Printed in the United States of America on acid-free paper.
10 9 8 7 6 5 4 3 2 1

Translator's Note

ARIANE, A Russian Girl is a very French novel that is also very Russian. Claude Anet spent most of the years 1917 to 1920 in Russia at the time of the Revolution, which he wrote about for the French press. The book was completed in Arkhangelsk, the Siberian city that was a center of White Russian resistance to the Bolsheviks.

The French have long tended to translate many foreign names into their language. Bach in France is known not as Johann Sebastian but as Jean-Sebastien, and Michelangelo is Michel-Ange. Anet often does the same in *Ariane*, giving characters the French versions of the more likely Russian names. Michel, for example, would have been Mikhail. In order to maintain the French flavor of Anet's Russia, the first names of characters have been left as they are in the original text. Anet also translated landmarks, leading his characters to attend a concert at the "Grand Theatre." That theater is more familiar to us as the Bolshoi, so in this and in similar cases the more familiar Russian names are used.

The editors and I would like to thank Robert Chandler for his assistance in these matters.

—M.A.

PART ONE

By Way of a Prologue

1. FROM THE HÔTEL DE LONDRES TO THE ZNAMENSKY GYMNASIUM

A SKY OF an almost oriental limpidity, a beautiful light-blue sky, radiant, as blue as a turquoise of Nishapur, was spread over the houses and gardens of the still sleeping city. Nothing could be heard in the dawn and the silence but the cries of sparrows chasing one another on the roofs and the branches of the locust trees, the voluptuous cooing of a turtledove in a treetop, and in the distance, the occasional shrill squeaking of the axles of a peasant cart moving slowly over the uneven paving stones of the Sadovaya, the main and most elegant street of the city. Near the immense, dusty, deserted cathedral square, a wooden fence enclosed the service courtyard of the Hôtel de Londres, whose flat, elongated facade, three stories tall, of stones as gray and gloomy as a rainy autumn day, stood flush with the Sadovaya, with neither balconies, pilasters, columns, or ornamentation of any kind.

The Hôtel de Londres, the best in the city, was renowned for its cuisine. Gilded youth, officers, industrialists, and nobility patronized its celebrated restaurant, where on afternoons and evenings until deep into the night, an orchestra of five skinny Jews and two little Russians played mediocre medleys from *Eugene Onegin* and *The Queen of Spades*, melancholy popular songs, and gypsy tunes with their staccato rhythms. So many festive gatherings were held here! So many sparkling dinners, so many "orgies"—to use the expression common

3

among us whenever parties at the Hôtel de Londres were spoken of—were held in this restaurant!

The hotel restaurant was made up of two rooms of unequal size. But there were no private dining rooms, so those wanting to dine far from the crowd were provided with special rooms with lounges on the second floor, which Leon Davidovich, the hotel doorman, always made sure were free for his customers.

This Leon, a Jew with squinty, dead eyes, was the house autocrat and one of the best-known figures in the city. Provincial notables sought his friendship and stopped in the vestibule to exchange a few friendly words with him. Leon was discreet, and what is the price of the silence and good graces of the doorman of such a well-known hotel? How many pink bills, even twenty-five-ruble bills, had he silently accepted, pale face impassive, bills slipped to him by the feverish hand of a man trembling with the idea of finding an asylum for a romantic rendezvous? One can't but think that there was a great number of people who wanted to ensure the secrecy of their happiness, for Leon Davidovich owned no fewer than three houses. Which proves that money flowed through the city, was earned with little difficulty, was spent with joy, and that life there burned like the blazing summer days on the plains of this southern *guberniya*, of which it was the capital. Every man who grew rich in the province, whether it was from the mines, from industry, or from agriculture, thought constantly of the unforgettable feasts of the Hôtel de Londres and the French wines that he would drink there in the company of charming women.

One of Leon Davidovich's three houses was located on an isolated street on the outskirts of town, not far from the road where, at dusk and during the night, beautiful trotting horses, the glory of our province, took couples eager to fly like the wind over a flat, even, and well-maintained road. The house was only two stories tall. Leon hoped to live there one day. For the moment he had furnished the second floor and had installed an old, repulsive woman there. Many had asked to rent it, for apartments were hard to come by in the city, which had developed with an extraordinary rapidity over the past few years. The crone's answer was always the same: the apartment was being held for someone. And yet no tenant ever arrived, and simple souls wondered why Leon deprived himself of a healthy rent. Others shook their heads. The fact is that in the evening people often saw a team of horses pull up at the door of the little house, and rays of light filtered through the carefully closed curtains far into the night.

In the early-morning hour when this tale begins, at the dawning of a hot day late in May, the main door of the Hôtel de Londres was closed and the lights had long since been turned off in the restaurant and the vestibule. The small wooden door in the gate of the service courtyard opened with a squeak. A young girl appeared on the threshold and stopped briefly, hesitant. She was wearing the uniform of the best known of the city's gymnasiums, a simple brown dress with an apron of black lustrine. She had lightened its severity with a white lace collar that looked a little wrinkled. Flouting the rules, the dress was slightly décolleté and revealed in all its delicate grace a long neck on which a tiny head swayed lightly, atop which was a wide-brimmed white straw hat tied under the chin by a black ribbon. The head tilted alertly to inspect the deserted street. The girl, after this brief pause, stepped onto the sidewalk. A second girl appeared behind her, a few years older, a bit heavy looking, wearing a black silk skirt and a batiste blouse under a light, demi-season coat.

The girl in the gymnasium uniform stretched, lifted her face to the sky, inhaled a breath of air as pure as a glass of cold water, and, laughing, said, "What a scandal, Olga. It's broad daylight."

"I wanted to go home a long time ago," the latter said grumpily. "I have no idea why you dawdled the way you did. Or rather, I know exactly why. And I have to be at the office at ten o'clock. That tyrant Petrov is going to make a scene. Plus I drank too much champagne."

The gymnasium student looked at her pityingly, but shrugged her left shoulder in a gesture customary to her, and said nothing. She walked rapidly, with a light, happy step, the too-high heels of her open-toed shoes clacking on the asphalt of the street, now bareheaded, gazing around, filled with the joy of finding the unexpected brightness of a spring dawn after leaving a smoke-filled room. They walked diagonally across the vast cathedral square and went their separate ways after having arranged to meet in the evening.

The gymnasium student followed a street to the left of the cathedral. Suddenly she heard the sound of hurried steps and turned around. A tall uniform-clad student wearing a cap sporting a gold appliquéd pick and shovel was running to catch up with her.

She stopped. Her face took on a harsh expression, her long eyebrows gathered in a frown, and the student, his eyes fixed on her, was immediately perturbed. He said nervously, "Excuse me, Ariane Nicolaevna. I waited till you were alone. I couldn't leave you like that after what happened—"

She cut him off, asking dryly, "Tell me, what happened?"

The young man's confusion was total. "I don't know," he mumbled. "I don't know how to tell you. It seemed to me ... You're angry with me, aren't you? I'm in despair ... I'd prefer to know right away. I can't live this way," he concluded, completely disconcerted.

"I'm not in the least angry with you," Ariane Nicolaevna answered, her voice clipped. "Know this once and for all: I never regret anything I've done. But remember, too, that I forbade you from approaching me on the street. I'm surprised you've forgotten."

He hesitated before the girl's icy gaze and then, turning on his heels, walked away, saying not a word.

A few minutes later Ariane Nicolaevna reached a large wooden house, its ground floor occupied by shops. She climbed to the second floor, the only one above street level, took a key from her handbag, and cautiously opened the door.

The silence of the apartment was disturbed only by the ticking of a large clock hanging on the kitchen wall. The girl crossed the long corridor on tiptoe and pushed open the door of a room where, on a narrow bed, a young chambermaid, her mouth hanging open, slept, half-dressed.

"Pasha, Pasha," she said.

The servant, startled awake, tried to rise from her bed.

"Call me at nine o'clock," Ariane said, pushing her back into bed. "At nine, do you hear? I have a test this morning."

"Very well, Ariane Nicolaevna. I won't forget. But it's broad daylight. How late you've come home! For the love of God, take care of yourself. Let me come undress you," she added, again trying to get out of bed.

"No, Pasha, don't bother yourself. Thank God I know how to dress and undress myself on my own. Given the way I live, it's something I need to know."

Seconds later, everything was at rest in the great house on the Dvoranskaya.

At ten o'clock in the morning that same day, in the famous gymnasium of which Mme Znamenskaya was the director, the history teacher Pavel Pavlovich, assisted by two other professors, was giving his students their school-leaving exam.

In the enormous room, well lit and bare, twenty girls were gathered. There were brief snatches of soft conversation among them, of whispered remarks, of short sentences heatedly exchanged. Burning eyes shone in pale faces; some of the students hastily flipped through the history textbook; others passionately followed what was going on at the rostrum.

The questioning lasted five minutes on a subject drawn at random, and during this time, the next student sat thinking at a small table off to the side. Ariane Nicolaevna waited for her turn, crumpling the letter she had just grabbed right in front of Pavel Pavlovich.

Two hours of sleep had sufficed to bring back her nearly childlike coloring. Her light gray eyes, on the small side, took shelter beneath her eyebrows, which nearly met at the beginning of her nose, which was straight, sharp, and well proportioned. Her delicately outlined mouth was closed. Ariane wasn't absorbed in meditation on the subject she was to be questioned on, but rather listened to the student who, standing before her examiners, provided only embarrassed answers. The gray eyes below the dark eyebrows sparkled, and it was clear that Ariane was making an effort not to fly to the assistance of her comrade.

A monitor sitting off to the side took out her watch and left. She returned two minutes later, escorted by the school's directress. The examiners fell over each other to offer her their seat. Mme Znamenskaya thanked them with a gesture and took the monitor's chair, towards the back of the room.

In the room a murmur passed from mouth to mouth. The girls softly offered their impressions.

"There she is again."

"She's always here when Ariane is questioned."

"It's scandalous the way she protects her."

Barely had the directress taken her seat when Pavel Pavlovich timidly knocked on the table and said to the student: "I thank you."

The girl descended from the rostrum and returned to her seat, her blushing face disappearing in her handkerchief.

In a hesitant voice the professor called, "Kuznetsova."

Ariane stepped forward.

His eyes lowered, the professor asked, "What is your subject?"

"Novgorod the Great."

And without waiting to be questioned, Ariane began her report. She spoke with an astounding correctness of expression. The most muddled question became clear when she dealt with it; the most confused subject seemed simple. She classified everything in keeping with its relative importance and, without losing herself in details, drew a luminous portrait in which every fact was laid out in an orderly fashion.

The examiners took as much pleasure in listening to her as they did in listening to a great artist in concert. Pavel Pavlovich didn't take his eyes off her, and the interest with which the directress followed the supple and precise words of Ariane Nicolaevna could be read on her impassive face. All eyes in the hall were turned to the rostrum.

"Five with a cross," said one.

"The prize for excellence and the gold medal," murmured another.

"Look at Pavel Pavlovich," a third whispered. "It's clear that he loves her."

"I've known that for a long time," a pale and serious young girl said.

The five minutes having passed, Pavel Pavlovich interrupted Ariane Nicolaevna. "That's enough, Kuznetsova. We thank you."

The girl stepped down from the rostrum. One of the examiners leaned towards a colleague. "That's a brilliant child," he said in a low voice.

An hour later the exam was over. While the students left the hall, Ariane Nicolaevna stayed behind and spoke with the directress. Their discussion went on for some time. Now they were alone. Finally, in a burst of tenderness that shocked the young girl, Mme Znamenskaya leaned towards her, kissed her, and said, "Wherever you might be, Ariane, never forget that I am your friend."

And then she left.

In the vestibule, two girls waited for Ariane Nicolaevna. They quickly stifled their whispers and giggles. One of them was tall, thin, and pale, with sparkling eyes and staccato movements. The other was homely, with tiny eyes and a flat nose, but stylish and fidgety. Both had bad reputations; they were sometimes seen wearing jewelry whose origin was deemed suspect, for they belonged to petty bourgeois families of modest fortune. They drew up alongside Ariane, and as they walked they caressed her, congratulated her, paid her a thousand compliments.

"Listen, Ariane," said the taller of them. "Do you want to come have supper with us this evening? We've arranged a party. It's in the new country house that Popov just bought." (This Popov was the wealthiest merchant in town, a man of a certain age, and quite repulsive looking.) "He set up the place in an interesting way. Imagine this: there are no chairs in the house, only sofas. I'm telling you, you really need to see this."

The small one excitedly cut in: "There are musicians he hides in the next room; you hear them, but they remain invisible. And there's a strange invention. The room is illuminated by candle ends that gradually go out, one after the other."

Ariane asked, "And who dines on these sofas? I don't see myself sitting next to Popov."

"Charming friends of his. And anyway, why don't you want to go to Popov's? He's head over heels in love with you, my dear. He dreams and talks only of you, Ariane Nicolaevna. You absolutely have to come with us."

"Thanks a lot," Ariane said. "Popov is horrible."

"But what wit! And you have to hear him sing. He's splendid; you wouldn't recognize him."

"Well, he'll sing without me," Ariane answered as she came to a stop, "for I'll see neither his country house nor his sofas nor his candle ends; not this evening or tomorrow. Tell him that for me."

"But he'll die of despair."

"Vodka will console him."

She left the girls, who continued on their way, troubled by the refusal and talking animatedly to each other.

The taller one said, "She wants to be begged. It's ridiculous."

And the small one: "Popov will not be happy."

Ariane entered a small garden, one that was more like an alley of trees and rosebushes running along the street. Pavel Pavlovich was feverishly pacing in it. He was gentle, inoffensive, dreamy, generous, and scared of everything, above all of being alone with Ariane Nicolaevna, even though they met in this garden two or three times a week after classes. But each time, Pavel Pavlovich was paralyzed by an emotion that nearly took away his ability to speak. That day, Ariane, after the brief conversation with her two friends, looked to be irritable, which only added to the teacher's dismay. And yet he was bold enough to ask her to sit on a bench off to the side. She refused: she was already very late and would reach home when lunch was over.

He accompanied her, complimenting her on her exam, repeating the flattering comment of one of the examiners: "A brilliant child."

Ariane, whose light head wobbled slightly on her svelte neck, straightened herself and whispered, "Child! How impertinent! I'm seventeen."

And she was again silent. Embarrassed, the teacher was silent as well. They walked briskly through the peaceful streets. For the first time that year it was already hot, foretelling the burning southern summer.

They reached the Dvoranskaya, and the house where

Ariane Nicolaevna lived. Pavel Pavlovich was paler than usual. Screwing up his courage, he began to speak.

Ariane interrupted him. "You know what I'm thinking about, Pavel Pavlovich? I look preoccupied, but I'm incredibly happy. Can you guess why? No? Well, I'll tell you. I am thinking of one thing and one thing alone. In a few minutes I'll be in my room. On my sofa I'll find a beautiful white dress, low cut and garlanded with Irish embroidery. And Pasha—do you know Pasha? She adores me. Whatever I do is good in her eyes. Pasha will have laid white silk stockings out with the dress and, near the sofa, open-toed white shoes. Then, Pavel Pavlovich, I will undress from head to toe. I'll throw this horrible gymnasium uniform onto the floor, this brown dress I haven't taken off for three years, and I'll dance on it, I'll trample it. And then I'll hug Pasha. This is all I'm thinking about. I'm free, free! Be happy for me."

She offered him her hands. Pavel Pavlovich listened to her and on his face could be read a battle of different emotions. The young girl's joy, her mere voice, intoxicated him. And yet he felt a vague sorrow.

Ariane had already left him and climbed onto the porch. In the doorway she turned. "If you have nothing better to do, come dine tonight at the Alexander Garden."

She vanished. Pavel Pavlovich remained motionless on the sidewalk.

2. AUNT VARVARA

WHEN ARIANE entered the large dining room, several people were seated at a table presided over by Aunt Varvara. She was a woman in her forties with an asymmetrical face in which one first noticed only a pair of big, dark, quite beautiful eyes, which on their own were enough to justify the common opinion in the city: "Varvara Petrovna is a seductive woman." Her coiffure was coquettish: her brown, slightly wavy hair was sharply parted. Her mouth was as clearly outlined as that of her niece, but her teeth were poor. Varvara Petrovna, who was aware of this, arranged things so that she smiled with her lips closed and with her shining brown eyes. Those who knew her said, "She's irresistible." She was still thin. "When Aunt Varvara walks down the street," Ariane would say, "the people behind her take her for a young girl." Even when she was home she dressed with care, something rare in Russia. Her shoes were elegant, her hands were well cared for, her linen delicate, and when outside, she unfailingly wore a fitted suit of black fabric, the work of a fine Moscow tailor.

Varvara Petrovna's life was an inexhaustible subject of interest for the residents of the city. Of her past it was recalled that she had left her family to study medicine in Switzerland after a series of incidents that remained obscure, returning to Russia as the local council physician in the town of Ivanovo in our *guberniya*.

At that time, in our house we were looking after her beautiful younger sister, Vera, who was spending the winter in the city and whom the novelist Kovalsky was head over heels in love with. At the very moment when everyone expected the announcement of the marriage of the young girl and the writer, the latter abruptly left for Crimea and the former for Ivanovo, hiding at her sister's house. No one saw her for six months, at which point she left for Paris, where, a year later, she married an engineer, Nicolas Kuznetsov, whose business often called him to Paris.

Shortly after her departure from Ivanovo it was discovered that Varvara's house sheltered an additional guest, a baby who Varvara said was a delicate child entrusted to her by a friend. This little girl hadn't been baptized in the village church, and when she was eighteen months old, Varvara took her abroad, where she spent some time with her married sister, Vera.

She returned alone. At this time, something occurred that changed the course of Varvara's life. One night she was called to the home of one of the largest landowners in Russia, Prince Y——, who by chance was spending a month on a nearby property. She saved his life. The prince grew attached to her, took her to Europe, and kept her by his side until his death seven years later. Varvara Petrovna then returned to her homeland with a fortune of 100,000 rubles, a pension of 10,000 rubles, and rich with the experience gained over the course of the brilliant life she'd led in the West. She purchased a house in the Dvoranskaya.

It was as if she'd never left Russia. She possessed, as if she had always practiced it, the art of passing time while doing nothing, and found the days too short without having anything with which to fill them. She rarely went into town; she spent barely a month each summer on a small property on the banks of the Don she'd acquired in order to have milk, eggs, and fresh vegetables. During her years of servitude at the side of the prince, she had exhausted her desire to travel, which is so deep-rooted in Russians. She regarded her past as one regards a stage set: as perhaps admirable, but a place where one wouldn't think of organizing one's life. One remains there for a few seconds under the artificial lights before the eyes of a thousand spectators, and then, after the performance, one returns home and closes the door.

This is what Varvara Petrovna did, but she left the door open a crack for the friends—the many friends, truth be told—she soon had in the city. She had been there for five years when her sister, Vera Kuznetsova, died from chest problems in San Remo. She had been alone there with her daughter, Ariane. Kuznetsov rushed to Saint Petersburg, brought his daughter back to Russia, and, not knowing what to do with her, proposed to his sister-in-law that she take her in.

When this news reached the house in the Dvoranskaya, Varvara's friends, talking among themselves, decided with no hesitation that she would refuse. How could she agree to burden herself, free as she was, with the education of a child she hardly knew? Varvara's friends were wrong. She had barely received her brother-in-law's letter when, without taking the time to reflect, she sent a telegram to Petersburg to say that her niece should be sent to her.

When Ariane arrived at her aunt's home she was a child of fourteen and a half, who, in body and mind, was older than her years. She was extremely thin but already formed,

her arms full and her face serious; her direct gaze had something aggressive about it.

"Who the devil do you resemble?" Varvara Petrovna asked
her. "You have our family's mouth, but you won't be as
beautiful as your mother. Where does that way of looking
at people come from? Who did you get those eyes from? Not
from your father, in any case. He's flabby and blind. You
don't have a single trait in common with him. For which I
congratulate you, since you know what I think of him ..."

This was the way Varvara Petrovna spoke. The girl's eyes
lit up, but she didn't answer.

"Anyway, I like you. I was afraid that you had remained
a child, but I see you're a young girl. We can speak freely."

Indeed, this child's presence brought no change to Varvara
Petrovna's existence. Despite the disparity in their ages, from
the first day she considered Ariane more a friend than a niece
whose education she had to see to.

As soon as she'd distanced herself from her family, Varvara
had gained the habit of and taste for freedom, and decided
she could dispose of herself as she saw fit. Since nature had
attached a secret and keen pleasure to the commerce of the
sexes, why should she deprive herself of it? Using the intelligent reasoning of a student, she found no excuse to refuse
herself such healthy joys. She had had lovers at the university;
upon returning to the country, she had even found some in
Ivanovo. During her travels abroad with the prince, she had
had many occasions to carry out comparative studies of the
merits of Westerners, and upon her return to her birthplace,
she continued to live in keeping with her tastes. She couldn't
understand the importance so many exalted people placed
on the giving of oneself. In a word, she looked on love the
way men did. She took a lover when the desire struck her

and left him when she found another more to her fancy. She didn't imagine that people unite in transports of passion or part in tears. In her eyes love was not a malady, and separation was no source of tragedy. She acted so naturally that her lovers never thought they had the right to ask for more than she gave them. In any case, she didn't leave them, and, with neither drama nor backlash, friendly relations succeeded the more intimate ones of love. On occasion she didn't say no to second go-rounds. During the first years of her settling in she had to go to Petersburg and Moscow several times. She had former boyfriends there and stayed at their homes. Upon her return, she recounted her trip and the pleasure she'd had without her lover of the moment taking offense.

As can be seen, Varvara Petrovna was a healthy and well-balanced woman. Her senses, to which she refused nothing, led her only halfway along the road of her passions. She loosened their bridle but they didn't run loose.

Her romantic morality—for she had one—was ruled by two principles. She remained faithful to her lover until the day a new man attracted her. She would immediately confess to this, for she wouldn't have understood sharing. She was a one-man woman, only who that man was changed often. As a result, she'd never cheated on anyone: in order to cheat on a man, you must love him, be attached to him with the bonds of sentiment. But until this time, Varvara had only seen in her lovers friends of a complementary sex, and the relations she established between them and herself were precisely defined. She flattered herself that she had in this way put love back in its proper place: no higher than the waist.

"You see, my dear," she said to Ariane Nicolaevna (who was barely fifteen and a half), "love is something delicious if you know how to take it as it is. Romanticism is the cause of all ills ... Anyway, I don't think you're threatened by that dangerous folly. You have a good head on your shoulders and you won't go astray."

The girl smiled her tight smile and kept her thoughts to herself.

Varvara Petrovna's second principle was that money should not be mixed with love. The morality of many Russian women on this point is the same as Varvara's. All is well when money plays no role, and whatever one might do, if one is disinterested, one remains an honest woman. Immorality begins with money. As a result, even when as a young girl in Geneva she'd had barely enough to live on, Varvara wouldn't have accepted a dinner or a tram ticket from her lover, even if he were rich. As was true for so many of her compatriots, there was some affectation in this.

When Ariane arrived from Petersburg, Varvara's boyfriend was a famous lawyer from a neighboring city who went to the provincial capital for business twice a week. When he came, he stayed at Varvara's house, where he had a room. Ariane had then seen him succeeded by an engineer. On the outside, everything happened harmoniously, but Varvara Petrovna never failed to tell her niece—become her confidant—the merits, failings, and peculiarities of her lovers.

"I'm doing you a service," she sometimes said. "You won't take foolish ideas into your head. You'll see things in their true light and you'll thank me later."

But over the past year Varvara had changed. Having passed forty, she had fallen for a doctor, whose beauty wreaked havoc on the city. At first Varvara had accepted Vladimir Ivanovich as she had so many others. The engineer had been summarily dismissed, and Vladimir Ivanovich had succeeded him. The first six months were enchanting, but Varvara then noticed the birth within herself of a feeling unknown to her. This discovery plunged her into simultaneous despair and rapture. She felt as if her entire life had crashed around her. She no longer recognized herself. Like a man who falls into a swamp and can't find a foothold, she didn't know what to hold on to. And at the same time, she was possessed by an unknown happiness. A tide of joy rose within her. She dreamed like a lovelorn seventeen-year-old.

"Ah," she said to Ariane, "I didn't know what happiness was. I've had eighteen lovers. What do I mean, 'lovers'? They were boyfriends, nothing more. And now, at forty, I meet Vladimir! To think that he lived right nearby and I didn't know him. I can't forgive myself for this. If you knew the kind of man he is..."

She went on and on. The young girl listened in silence, still smiling, but now her teeth nibbled at her lower lip.

Having known love, Varvara soon felt its storms. She thought she'd noticed that Vladimir Ivanovich no longer had the same feelings for her as he'd had at the beginning.

To be sure, he saw her every day, but he came at times that hadn't been designated for him in the past: at dinnertime, for example, or in the evening for tea. Sometimes he even showed up at six o'clock, when Varvara took her daily stroll. He didn't linger as he had at the beginning of their relationship. He rarely spent the evening in the small sitting room next to Varvara's bedroom. It was only with difficulty that she managed to get him to enter. He preferred to sit in the dining room, where, along with Ariane, there could always be found her oldest friend, Olga Dimitrievna, who for some time took her meals at Varvara's house, along with several habitués.

He had no trouble making up excuses: his wife had returned from the countryside, or she was ill; he had patients to visit, or a migraine...

Varvara Petrovna was distraught. This woman, who had made it a point of honor never to ask for anything, lowered herself to beg for rendezvous or even a few moments more of his presence, doing so even in front of her niece and her friends.

Varvara was tortured by jealousy. Vladimir must have a new mistress. She took to spying on him. She scrutinized him carefully, and reflected. She observed his looks, noted his intonation when he spoke. She who never went out in the morning took to running around the city, passing in front of her lover's house a hundred times a day. She went so far as to follow him in a coach. But who knows what a fashionable doctor does?

She had lost the joy and carefree attitude of a happy woman upon whom fortune smiles and who has nothing to do but live her life.

That day, when Ariane returned from her final exam, Varvara was still sitting at the table, though lunch was long since over.

"Did your exam go well?"

Before the girl could answer, Vladimir Ivanovich appeared. It seemed as if he had watched out for Ariane in order to follow right after her. He was an active man, always on the run, nearly fifty, clean shaven and with graying hair. He had the most beautiful teeth in the world and the most sparkling eyes, beneath bristling long, dark eyebrows. His least gesture expressed extreme assurance. Varvara abruptly rose and offered him her hand.

"How late you are," she said.

Vladimir Ivanovich kissed Varvara's hand and, immediately pulling away from her, hurried over to Ariane, who hadn't moved.

"I came expressly to congratulate you, Ariane Nicolaevna. My daughter told me that you had a triumph. I never doubted it, in any event."

He squeezed Ariane's hand between his. She briskly pulled it away. Varvara noted this gesture. "Please sit, Vladimir Ivanovich," she said. "I'll pour you some coffee."

"No, I don't have any time. I have a thousand errands to run."

"You'll drink a cup of coffee; I'm not going to allow you to leave. And perhaps I'll go out with you to get some fresh air. Today's the first day of summer. What are you going to do, Ariane?"

"I'm staying here until seven," the girl answered. "Nicolas is going to pick me up in a coach. I'm tired, so I'm going to take a nap."

"I almost forgot," Varvara said. "There's a letter for you from your father in your room."

Ariane frowned. Her face grew somber whenever her father's name was mentioned.

A few minutes later, no one was left in the dining room.

3. THE LETTER

WHEN ARIANE entered her room she saw her father's letter in the middle of the table, and recognized his careful handwriting. It had been sent by registered post. She shrugged.

Before reading it she undressed from head to toe and tossed her brown uniform onto a chair. She undid her auburn hair, long and full, put on a light robe, grabbed the letter, and stretched out barefoot on the sofa.

The letter began:

My Dear Daughter,

In response to your letter of the tenth of this month [this businesslike expression brought a grimace to her youthful face], I'm letting you know my plans. It doesn't suit me that you enter the university. Without you we already have enough déclassé women in Russia. You're intelligent and you'll use your intelligence when you're married in raising your children. I hope you'll wed soon. Our friend Pierre Borisovich, whom you probably remember, thinks of you fondly and his greatest desire is to marry you. As you know, he's a serious boy who can assure you the most agreeable of lives. Even more, he has a post of the first order in business, and I can answer for him as much as I can for myself. I'm going to the Caucasus for a month to take the waters.

I'm counting on you when I return to Petersburg in September. We'll spend the fall in Pavlovsk, where Pierre Borisovich has a charming villa...

It went on like this for four pages.

The young girl couldn't read any farther. She crumpled the letter. "Disgusting!" she said. And she tossed it into the corner.

Then she closed her eyes and daydreamed for a few seconds. She saw herself again at age eight, sitting on the lap of her godfather, Prince Vyaminsky. What a strange man. How he loved her! He seemed to live for her alone. When she went to see him he would alternate between giving her brand-new beautiful gold pieces and exquisite chocolate candies. She ate the chocolates immediately; the gold pieces she hid in her schoolbag, since her mother would never have allowed her to accept them. So when she went to school, she carried thirty coins which, even wrapped in silk paper, softly jingled with every step. This godfather, she later learned, had asked to adopt her. He had wanted to raise her as he pleased and to have her always at his side. He had very white, very cold hands; she shivered when he caressed her arms or her cheeks... Everything grew blurry before her.

In the silent room the yellow blind covering the window was illuminated in golden light cast by the rays of the setting sun.

She continued to dream... The prince was at her side. She slept, but saw him through her closed eyelids. He gazed at her with such intensity that it oppressed her. And suddenly— how did this happen?—she felt her godfather's cold hand on her lower leg.

She opened her eyes and saw Vladimir Ivanovich seated

on the sofa upon which she was lying. His hand was resting on her naked ankle and, sitting stock-still, he was gazing at the young girl. As soon as he saw she was awake, he leaned towards her.

"Excuse me, Ariane Nicolaevna, excuse me. I knocked on your door and since no one answered I came in. I've been here for some time already—"

She didn't let him finish. "Your hands are cold," she said, "like my godfather's. It's horrible! You will let go of my ankle immediately."

As she spoke she closed her bathrobe, which was hanging open, not taking her eyes off Vladimir Ivanovich. Her tone didn't allow for any contradiction, and the doctor removed his hand.

"And get off the couch immediately."

The frail young girl spoke with such authority that Vladimir Ivanovich rose.

Ariane unhurriedly sat up, got off the sofa, slid her feet into her slippers, walked to the door, opened it, and said with calm assurance, "And now leave! Believe me, it's for the best. I didn't know that it was for me that you came to this house."

The doctor took her hand, pulled her towards him, and, his face close to hers, softly said, "Think what you will of me, the truth is that I can't live without seeing you. I have to talk to you . . . Come to my house someday."

"And you'll invite your daughter, who's the same age as me, to witness our conversation," Ariane said defiantly.

Vladimir Ivanovich was struck dumb, but regained his wits. "I am always alone at seven o'clock in the lodge where I see patients. I'll be waiting for you."

"Right, it's true. You're a doctor. If things go on this way, that could be useful. I'll keep you in mind if it's necessary, Vladimir Ivanovich."

He stepped back. His eyes shone, but without responding, he left.

A few seconds later, as she was getting dressed, there were three discreet knocks on the door, which opened, letting in Olga Dimitrievna.

She had lived with Varvara for a long time, but after getting a job at city hall, and wishing to be more independent, she now rented a small room, where she slept. But she was daily at Varvara Petrovna's home, where she dined and spent the evening with Ariane Nicolaevna, to whom she was very attached. Whether her feelings were reciprocated is not clear. In any case, the two girls were rarely apart and shared all their secrets, though Olga was five years older than her friend. This character trait of Ariane's must be pointed out: owing to a certain self-assurance, she was the equal of friends and family far older than she. We have already seen a striking example of this in Ariane's relations with her aunt. Olga hid nothing of her secret life from Ariane, and that blond, exuberant girl was certain that she knew everything about her friend. But if a clear-eyed observer had witnessed the lively conversations of the two young girls, he would have noted the way Ariane sometimes looked at her confidant, and sought an explanation. The close relations between Ariane and Olga provided the latter with certain benefits. Despite her extreme youth, Ariane had been able to gather around her a court of admirers eager to fulfill her every fantasy, and many a strange one passed through her head. Picnics, suppers, sledding parties, and dances—Olga participated in all kinds of festivities, and it wasn't possible to invite Ariane without her friend. She played the unflattering role of chaperone, but arranged matters in such a way as to draw advantages that are not part of the tradition of secondary characters.

Once she was in the room, she looked at Ariane and said, with a mix of pique and admiration, "I don't understand a thing. You dined, you drank champagne, you did God knows what, you rested barely two hours, you took an exam, and now here you are, as fresh as if you'd slept all night."

"Add, dear friend, that I have problems," Ariane said. "I finally received a response from my father. Everything is finished between us. Here, read his letter."

She offered the crumpled paper to Olga, who read it closely.

When Olga finished, she looked at her friend, who sat at her night table fixing her hair.

"So..."

"So," Ariane answered, "I'll do without him. It's not hard to find money in a city like ours."

Olga Dimitrievna ran to her. She was upset. "I know who you're thinking of," she said, "but it's impossible. Swear to me that you won't do it. I can't bear the idea... You'll only harm yourself."

She leaned over her friend, took her in her arms, and hugged her, her eyes full of tears.

"Speak to your aunt, to Nicolas, to the devil, but not to you-know-who. Promise me."

Ariane gently pushed her away. "First let me do my hair. That's the only thing that matters. You so love to be dramatic. And now you're crying... Is this your business or mine? Who's going to suffer, you or me? You know that I can never discuss money with my aunt. That's just the way she is and there's nothing I can do about it, We love each other very much and I'm not going to spoil what's excellent between us for a wretched question of interest. No, let me arrange things the way I want."

She stood up and leaned affectionately on Olga's shoulder as she wiped her eyes. "You're so silly, my poor child. Go light a candle for me at the church and stop worrying. I won't be as easily devastated as you think. Do you remember what trial by fire was in the Middle Ages? You had to pass through flames without being burnt. Well, you can be certain that I'll pass through it and the flames won't touch me."

She paced back and forth in the room, which was filled with a grave silence. Suddenly she stopped in front of Olga Dimitrievna and with a gleeful air said, "Do you know who just left? Vladimir Ivanovich, my dear!"

Seeing Olga Dimitrievna's incredulous look, she told of her surprising awakening and the scene that followed, not failing to include a certain number of dramatic and piquant details that honored her imagination more than they did her veracity.

Olga listened with passionate curiosity, and when the tale was over she sighed and said, "He's so seductive ... He was here, on this sofa! I wouldn't have been able to resist him."

They spoke at length on this inexhaustible subject. Pasha interrupted them, announcing that dinner was served.

Before the meal was over, Ariane rose and made her excuses to her aunt. "Nicolas is waiting for me downstairs," she said. And turning to Olga: "I'll be back at nine and we'll go to the Alexander Garden together."

4. THE FIANCÉ

A SMALL victoria with pneumatic tires, harnessed to a pair of beautiful black horses of the famous race of trotters raised in the province, was parked in front of the house. Pacing the sidewalk was a tall, corpulent young man, brown haired, bearded, taking hurried puffs on cigarettes that he immediately flicked away. Every few minutes he would stop, look up at the second-floor veranda, check his watch, and resume walking. Nicolas Ivanov was known in town as two things and two things alone: as a horse lover and as the unilateral and capricious fiancé of the already famous Ariane Nicolaevna. He was a strange and unsociable boy, rarely seen and friendless, who spent most of the year on a property thirty versts away. In town he had only a two-room pied-à-terre in a bourgeois apartment. He didn't drink, he didn't play cards, and he wasn't known to have any romantic relations. His father was long dead and his mother lived in Crimea. It was said that her mind was unhinged and that she was held in the clinic of a well-known doctor. As a result of living alone, Nicolas Ivanov had become taciturn and had real difficulty speaking. He would hunt for words, start over again, contradict himself, and stop in the middle of a sentence, until finally lapsing into the silence that was so agreeable to him. His appearance was more or less pleasing, with big blue eyes beneath dark brown eyebrows and hair. But his coloring was pale and his gaze worried. Mothers and young girls had long tried to capture this rich prey, for it was thought Nicolas Ivanov possessed nearly one million rubles. Their efforts had been in vain.

One evening he had allowed himself to be dragged to the annual ball given by the Znamensky Gymnasium.

Ariane was on the organizing committee of the event and had offered him a flower upon his arrival. Nicolas had taken the flower, stared at length at the young girl in a way that embarrassed her as he mumbled his thanks, and finally dogged her steps throughout the evening. When she danced he looked at her with a tender smile, and, before leaving the dance hall, he hurried to the buffet and gulped down several glasses of wine as if to buck up his courage. Towards the end of the evening, in a burst of heroic intrepidity, he asked Ariane to marry him. Ariane—she was sixteen—looked him over from head to toe with the greatest insolence and laughed in his face. But the next day he showed up at the house of Varvara Petrovna, who tried in vain to explain to him that her niece was not old enough to marry. Two days later he brought an engagement ring engraved with Ariane's name and the date of the ball. He announced to the whole town that as soon as she finished classes, Ariane Nicolaevna Kuznetsova would become Mme Nicolas Ivanova. After that, flowers were brought every day to Ariane Nicolaevna, who eventually conceded that the beautiful flowers and the rare coach rides she granted Nicolas Ivanov were quite pleasant.

There's no way to give an idea of the capricious despotism under which this child of sixteen held that colossus almost twice her age. What is strange is that it wasn't gradually that she had become aware of her absolute power over him. From the first day she had understood who was standing before her and that Nicolas would be putty in her childish fingers. She regulated his visits and their duration. Nicolas came to see her only at the hours she dictated. God forbid that he should dare present himself without permission at the house on the Dvoranskaya! One day, for I don't know what pressing reason, he showed up in the dining room unexpectedly. Without saying a word, Ariane went to her room and refused to receive him. She often forced him to spend a week or two in the country without being allowed to write to her. She occasionally permitted him to accompany her to the theater, where she was a regular and where she rarely missed a performance, for she was mad about the theater, frequented actors, declared that she would become an actress herself, and that the only life that counted was that of the stage. Sometimes, in the middle of the evening she would walk across the stage and talk to the actors in their dressing rooms, forgetting Nicolas, who would return home alone, grumbling through clenched teeth.

She once tried the following experiment. One winter evening at ten o'clock, when Nicolas was having his tea in his room, she said to him, "I'm going out, Nicolas. I have an appointment."

"I'll accompany you," he said. "Where are you going?"

"A friend is waiting for me at the corner of the church square, but you can't know who."

He looked at her in astonishment. And then, after a moment, making an effort to control himself, he said, "Fine."

They went out together, and when she saw in the light cast by the streetlamp the young man she was looking for, she bid Nicolas adieu, telling him to return to his home immediately.

To top it all off, it must be noted that Nicolas was desperately jealous, and he found a thousand excellent reasons to believe that Ariane was involved in intrigues, the best one being that the girl made no mystery about this and spoke to him about it constantly. For example, she'd say to him, "Nicolas, do you know who's just arrived from Moscow? Maklakov's eldest son. I think I'm in love with him. He's irresistible..." And a hundred like statements, around the clock.

On the day after she'd had Nicolas accompany her to a rendezvous with another, Ariane, laughing out loud, told her confidant about it. However used to her friend's caprices the latter was, she couldn't hold herself back from saying, "Ariane, you're really mean."

Ariane stopped laughing and responded seriously, "So I'm mean. Why shouldn't I be if it amuses me?"

The chubby blond was stunned.

Ariane continued, "Do you want me to tell you something that you'd never find out on your own? It's precisely because I'm mean that Nicolas loves me. And you, who are as nice as can be—he'll never love you."

With this she started dancing around her room, because she was, despite her other qualities, quite childlike. She stuck her tongue out at people on the street, played practical jokes on her classmates, and exasperated her teachers with her ungovernableness.

What is most surprising is that Ariane was right. Nicolas Ivanov—the only and spoiled child of a wealthy family, who never encountered any obstacles to his caprices, to which no one had ever said no, who had never had anything but easy pleasures with accommodating women—had initially looked with amazement, as if she were an incomprehensible phenomenon, upon this frail young girl who spoke to him commandingly. He had immediately obeyed for the simple reason that he didn't feel within himself the strength to resist the mysterious power that emanated from Ariane. During his long hours of solitude he had endlessly turned this strange problem over in his mind. Why did he accept the slavery Ariane condemned him to? And, more important, why did she act this way with him? The solution had suddenly come to him: "She subjects me to such trials only to be sure of my love. And if she multiplies the trials it's because I am not not a matter of indifference to her. If she didn't love me, she'd leave me in peace. If she torments me, it's because she loves me. She's an admirable girl."

And so the more Ariane made him suffer, the more grateful he was and the fonder of her he became. He reached a point where he couldn't even conceive of disobeying the girl's whims. And the harsher the test, the happier he was to vanquish himself and so to win the love of this peerless girl. The day after he accompanied her to her rendezvous with a rival, he kneeled before her and said, "Ariane, I thank you. Yesterday you gave me the greatest proof of love a man could ask for. Be blessed..."

In response, the young girl shrugged and did a pirouette.

She played another game with him, one even more terrible.

Of an evening she would occasionally allow him to take tea in her room. They would converse at length. Nicolas would then find the ability to speak, sometimes eloquently. She would have him sit alongside her on the sofa, and would gaze at him brightly and tenderly. The pudgy boy would soon put his arm around her thin, uncorseted waist, move gradually closer to the girl, and his lips would end up resting on the bare, round, firm arm of Ariane and devouring it with kisses.

Half-stretched across the sofa, she seemed not even to notice; it was as if she were absent from the scene.

"Do you love me?" Nicolas ventured with a sigh.

"*Nichevo*, don't worry yourself," the girl said in an untranslatable tone.

Finally, Nicolas, no longer able to control himself, attempted a decisive attack. Ariane slipped out from between his fingers. "It's too hot in here for you. You're going to be sick. Go get some fresh air, Nicolas."

And to make sure that he had no choice but to do so, she went into the dining room, where Olga Dimitrievna was drinking her tea with one of the house's regulars.

Nicolas fled like a hurricane without saying goodbye to a soul, leapt into his coach, and gave the order to speed ten versts down the road. On freezing winter nights he left his cloak open, and the coachman, from his seat, heard the *barine* cast incomprehensible exclamations into the night.

"To the devil with her!" he was shocked to hear. "I'll kill her... Faster, faster!... Bitch!... I adore you!"

That evening, for the first time that year, the air was as warm as a summer's night. The coach sped along, and the girl, huddled in her corner under a greatcoat of black silk that hid her white dress, sat there numb, not feeling the pressure of Nicolas's arm around her waist. The slim crescent moon shone to the east. When the road passed through a copse of acacias, the sharp smell of clusters of buds suddenly enveloped Ariane. Then there was the subtler perfume of the meadows of high grass extending into the distance on both sides of the road. The mildness of the atmosphere, the somber limpidity of the gold-flecked sky, the silence of the natural world acted as a balm on the girl's irritated nerves. She forgot her companion; her mind was a blank; she silently enjoyed the calm of this beautiful evening.

Nicolas sat in silence. He finally hazarded a few sentences. Not receiving a response, he screwed up his courage and became more explicit. He told Ariane that from that day forward she was free; that she had concluded both the gymnasium and a period of her life covered in glory. There was finally nothing standing in the way of the projects they had contemplated for eighteen months; all that was left was to set the date of their wedding. What did she want to do after the ceremony? Travel abroad? Remain on his land? Go to Crimea? He awaited her decision.

The young girl remained absorbed in thought. Nicolas grew worried. "Answer me, I beg you," he said anxiously.

She turned towards him and, looking him in the eyes, said, "Don't torment me, Nicolas. I'm unhappy… I'll tell you more in a few days. Now let's go back."

The chubby boy was shattered. Ariane had never spoken to him this way before. She had never said as much about herself as she did in those four sentences. He had a dark feeling that something tragic he couldn't conceive of was in the offing. What had happened? Ariane, queen of the world, was surrendering, was unhappy. She had appealed to his pity… This was beyond his understanding. He felt dizzy. Tears suddenly rose to his eyes and he broke down in sobs.

The girl placed her hand on his feverish one. They returned home this way, not speaking a word.

At the door she said in the same gentle tone, "Goodbye. I'll call you in a few days."

5. THE ALEXANDER GARDEN

THE ALEXANDER Garden was the pride of the city. Located barely ten minutes from the cathedral, it offered many charms. A society composed of town notables ran it for the benefit of all. The admission price was fifty kopecks, twenty-five with a membership. At its center was a bicycle track with banked curves and two tennis courts surrounded by wire netting. At one end of the terrace overlooking the track was an open-air theater, which offered operettas and light comedies in the summer. At the other end was a restaurant whose vast rooms opened onto flowered balconies. The restaurant was managed by the owner of the Hôtel de Londres, who, as soon as good weather set in, relocated his famous chef and his mediocre orchestra there. On summer nights the terrace, the theater, and the restaurant glowed under lights. Officers and functionaries, merchants and industrialists, met their wives, their sons, their daughters, and their mistresses there. Actresses strolled there after shows. A thousand intrigues began and ended between the theater and the restaurant in the harsh light of the electric globes. Farther along, alleys disappeared into the shadows and offered a cover to couples wishing to hide. In the dark, passionate whispers, gay and stifled laughter, hurrying steps could be heard...

That evening, the two girls crossed the long terrace packed with a lively crowd and exchanged greetings left and right, but didn't stop. When they had almost reached the restaurant, a man seated in the shade of the balcony rose and approached them. Olga Dimitrievna gave a start. "Naturally he's here," she said, clutching her friend's arm to drag her away.

But Ariane stopped and offered her hand to the man, who was coming to meet her. He was of average height, with a round, chubby face and small blinking eyes set between slightly heavy lids. His ashen coloring bespoke poor health. He wore a mustache cut à l'anglaise, and the hair on both sides of his head was closely cut, while his skull was completely bald. His hands were heavy and puffy. He was ageless and walked quite slowly, leaning on a cane as he did so. He had retired from business several years before. He was a mass of obsequiousness, holding your hand in his, taking you by the shoulder, leaning into you as he spoke, his interlocutor re-treating to avoid unpleasant contact. Michel Ivanovich Bog-danov was well read, refined, and of a curious turn. But there was something disturbing about him that was difficult to define, though it could be clearly felt. He had been much spoken about, without anything specific ever having been alleged. Then his name was mixed up in a painful affair that had occurred in the city the previous year. One of the most charming of the society girls had committed suicide at eigh-teen. The causes of the suicide were unknown. It was one of those cases of disgust with life so frequent among Russian youths, whose nerves, both agitated and weak, are often unable to resist life's first shocks. Letters from Bogdanov had been found at the girl's house; obscure, very literary letters from which no conclusion could be drawn except that an intimate relationship—perhaps of only a spiritual sort—existed between her and Bogdanov. Society, peeved by this enigma, held Michel Ivanovich responsible for the suicide and gave him the cold shoulder. It was precisely during this time, doubtless out of defiance, that Ariane saw him often and had long conversations with him, though only in public. Michel Ivanovich seemed to take great pleasure in them. Ariane's sparkling wit dazzled him. He always spoke to her respectfully, not as if to a girl, but as if to a woman of great culture with whom one can freely discuss the most elevated questions. He led her to believe, without openly saying so, that in him she would always have, above and outside all of society's conventions, the most devoted friend, and that among people of their intellectual class there were no barriers, which were constructed only to keep out the mob. There emanated from these elevated conversations a fairly materialistic point of view on life, which could be summed up as follows: that money played a great role in one's existence; that at any given moment one might have need of it and be forced to quickly find some; that no one is protected against the blows of fate; and that if Ariane Nicolaevna ever found herself needing some, he, Michel Ivanovich, would be only too happy to make it available to her, since he had it in abundance. This was never formulated as crudely as I do here; not a word had been expressed that might shock Ariane Nicolaevna and cause her to halt her interlocutor, who was able to make himself understood without ever clearly explaining himself. In any case, from their many conversations there was no mistaking that he offered his services and that she understood this. All of it, of course, was drowned in a flood of subtle and ethereal words that made the most material questions something supersensible, something outside the world of interests, something resembling a commerce of the soul, like a sublime negotiation of spiritual affairs.

Ariane's unerring instincts had not misled her. Michel

Ivanovich was at her disposal if she ever had need of him. As for the price to be paid for his services, it goes without saying that there was never a question of this. Did Ariane ever even contemplate this, given that Michel Ivanovich's propositions seemed destined to remain perpetual wishes? The girl was flattered to see the enigmatic character who fascinated the entire town added to her mass of slaves. Bogdanov was a man of broad intelligence, and the homage he rendered her had a rare savor.

Followed by Olga Dimitrievna, who would not have left her friend's arm for all the money in the world, she led the engineer far from the terrace to a dark alley.

With her usual directness, she immediately addressed what was on her mind. "You know that I will perhaps have need of you?"

"Incomparable friend," he answered (he loved to speak in this fashion, which emphasized even more all that was outdated and ridiculous in what he was saying), "you know that I am entirely yours, entirely... too happy to be at your service."

"Well then, I want to go to the university and I'm having difficulties with my family."

"Family, family... An abominable yoke... In truth, a form of slavery. A mind like yours, Ariane Nicolaevna... What suffering! I thank you for having thought of me. I am touched, truly touched. But there's something you don't seem to have thought of." He took the girl's hand in his own and held it. "How could I accept losing you? What would become of me without you in this barbarous city? I could not resign myself to renouncing the precious moments you grant me." He whispered so close to Ariane's face that Olga Dimitrievna could barely make out his words. "In any case, we must think about this, speak about it, speak about it at length. You'll call me on the telephone, won't you? Whenever you wish ... Rest assured that I will be there for you, and I thank you from the bottom of my heart."

Ariane withdrew her hand. She hesitated briefly and then, turning to Olga Dimitrievna, said, "Wait for me here; I'll be back in a minute."

Leaving her friend stunned, she moved off into the shadows with the engineer. "Michel Ivanovich," she said, "I don't know why I address myself to you. I'm not thinking. Perhaps I'm wrong ... But I like things to be clear and we have to speak honestly. I'll need money to go to the university. Can you lend it to me? I say 'lend' because I have several tens of thousands of rubles left to me by my mother, which will be mine when I am of age. Will you be my banker? It's a business deal I am proposing to you, a simple business deal. I ask that you look on it as that and nothing more. I don't want to owe anything to anyone, so it must be treated as I intend or not at all. And I need an immediate response. Can you lend me money and what interest do you want on the sum you'll advance me?"

"But my friend, my precious friend," Michel Ivanovich responded, "I don't understand. Truly, I'm confused. A business arrangement between you and me? That's impossible. How could you even think of that? You, Ariane Nicolaevna, need a miserable few thousand rubles? Then they're yours, with no conditions, none! My sole reward will be thinking that my unworthy self was able to contribute to the development of your rare personality. It's an honor, a great honor for me. But I must admit that I tremble at the thought of losing you. My poor health prevents me from spending time in Petersburg or Moscow. I have to be sure that you won't forget me, that you'll return here every year during your vacation and that you'll take care of me as if I were an invalid. It's true that I'm a sick man, a sick man who doesn't ask for much...Just a few hours of conversation with you every week. You can't know this, Ariane Nicolaevna, but the only days when I feel alive are those when you deign to chat with me. The charms of your wit are an incomparable remedy for all my ills. The mere sound of your voice gives me strength. It's a miracle, a veritable miracle! And since you allow me to say so, I suffer cruelly at seeing you so little, by chance, in a crowd and always with your friend, who is charming but whose intelligence can't be compared to yours. If you pitied me you would grant me a few hours of conversation, calm conversation, far from hangers-on, at my home. It would be an act of charity. You have a gift of life that is so precious, my friend, that you even communicate it to the dying! Do you know what I call you? The Queen of Sheba. Yes, you remember, the Queen of Sheba in *La Tentation de Saint Antoine*, 'who had many tales to tell, each more amusing than the others.' Everything you tell me about your marvelous childhood, of your days among us, I consider more colorful than the most beautiful tales of the Orient. This is the sole grace I ask of you."

Ariane, in the driest of tones, which contrasted strangely with the extreme emotion of Michel Ivanovich's pathos, said to him, "And how many times will I be 'the Queen of Sheba' at your house until my departure?"

Michel Ivanovich was stunned into silence. "But my friend—" he began.

"Tell me straight, please. I want to know all the conditions of the bargain."

"I can't bear to hear you talk this way... A bargain! You've completely misunderstood."

"If you don't answer immediately, I'll leave and we'll never speak of the matter again."

Michel Ivanovich hesitated. "I don't know, two or three times a week."

"Let's say twice. And how many hours will I spend telling you tales?"

"Really, you're cruel; these details are horrible."

"Well, then I'll settle it myself. It'll be twice a week for an hour. Those are your conditions. It's expensive . . . Let me think about it. Goodbye."

He held her back. "One more word. I'm moving. I wasn't happy at my place. It's too noisy. And besides, I've lived there a long time; it's full of memories. Did you know that I can't live surrounded by memories? They bombard me . . . I'm a sick man, Ariane Nicolaevna; please understand that. I've rented a small house in the suburbs, peaceful, isolated, the little house that belongs to Leon—yes, to the concierge at the Hôtel de Londres. I'll have it to myself."

Michel Ivanovich was already moving off, leaning on his cane, dragging his leg.

The supper brought together a dozen people on a restaurant terrace. Ariane and Olga were the only two young ladies. Pavel Pavlovich was there, and the tall blond young man who had met Ariane on the street that same morning at five o'clock as she was leaving the Hôtel de Londres. That evening, Ariane's favorite, seated to her right, was a student with a small delicate face and hair as dark as night, but whose eyes were blue and whose teeth were marvelously white. They had moved on from vodka to champagne. Olga Dimitrievna gazed tenderly at her neighbor; with her hand resting on his, she assured him in caressing tones that she was oh, so sad and that her soul was sick. Ariane sparkled with life and wit. She had never been as joyful, as brilliant. She stood up to everyone, and epigrams as sharp as arrows issued from her bow-shaped lips.

But suddenly, when the conversation turned to honesty in love, her tone changed, and with a new intonation remarked on by all, she said, "What's honesty? A girl who gives herself for money has her honesty, just like a woman who has no lover. Who can measure from without where honesty is, and where shame? It's a sentiment buried deep within us and of which we alone are judge . . . I could sell myself," she said, looking directly at Olga Dimitrievna—who gave a start, "and remain honest in my own eyes."

"What are you saying?" the blond young man interjected anxiously.

"Yes," said Ariane. "Suppose that I should be without money and feel within myself an implacable need, an obligation to expand my intelligence, to go to the university, to participate in the high culture for which I was born. I can't even think of ruining the ideal I pursue by wasting my time giving lessons to little imbeciles for two rubles an hour. I need money. Whom should I ask for it? The lover I love? Impossible: you don't mix money and love. But if a man I don't love, for the few hours he'll have my body, assures me of the possibility of a rich and spiritual life, isn't it my duty to accept this bargain? Don't I remain honest and faithful to myself by accepting the deal and paying with the only coin I possess? The world might condemn me, but what's the world? A gathering of fools and a pile of prejudices. Let it judge me as it will. But in my eyes I remain an honest girl."

Half the company applauded furiously. Pavel Pavlovich lowered his head.

"She's right!" someone cried.

"Now that's real human morality," said another. "Bravo!"

Olga Dimitrievna's neighbor, from whose hand she'd briskly wrested her own, leaned towards her. She was crying. "What's wrong?" he asked.

"Please, don't pay any attention," she said. "It's my nerves. But keep talking to me so the others don't see my tears."

6. TROUBLED DAYS

THE REGULARS at the Dvoranskaya were worried, for Varvara Petrovna's mood was undergoing strange modifications. She had formerly been the gayest, the most amiable, the most carefree, the most even-keeled of women. But now Varvara, whose charm resided in the smiling disposition that seemed to be as much a part of her as her beautiful black hair and the smile that caused people to lose their heads, was now, depending on the time of day, nervous, worried, agitated, or lacking in self-control. She, who never said a hurtful word to anyone, now said the most disagreeable things to her oldest friends, who looked at one another, terrified, fearing a catastrophe.

Vladimir Ivanovich, the handsome doctor with the graying hair, still frequented her home. But he came and went, sitting at the table for a few minutes when Varvara had guests. If he entered the small sitting room that adjoined the bedroom, it was with a cigarette in his mouth, on the fly. He no longer spent long hours at her side as he once had. And he, too, had lost the unshakable calm and self-assurance of the past.

Varvara's behavior with Ariane was strange. Sometimes she smothered her with caresses; she kept her close under any pretext, prevented her from leaving, gave her gifts. At other times, on the contrary, she attacked her in public, or pushed her away and, after spending entire days without speaking to her, seemed no longer to know her. The young girl accepted these fickle moods with indifference and seemed not to notice either her aunt's tenderness or her anger.

One day, when the latter was in one of her spells of gaiety and expansiveness, Ariane—this was shortly after the school-leaving exam at the gymnasium—broached the subject of her proposed departure for the university and laid out the problems she was having with her father. Varvara was not fond of her brother-in-law, whom she never saw.

"Your father has always been a fool, my dear," she said. "And you are far too intelligent to live with him. As for his project to marry you off, it's absurd. You're nothing but a child. What do you know of life? Do you even have a lover?"

Laughing, she stopped, observed her niece, and continued. "In fact, do you have a lover? You know everything I do: I've never hidden a thing from you. But when I think about it, what do I know about you? Speak, you little mask."

The girl smiled but said nothing. Varvara went on: "You have the city at your feet. You drive men mad. But what do you give of yourself? And yet all I need do is look at you and I can see that you are blood of our blood. At your age your mother had lived a novel. Myself, when I was eighteen, I lived however it pleased me. And I've been assured that the young girls of today have made great progress and have left us behind. Come, come. For once, speak frankly: What do you do to men? I see that you lead them wherever you want. Oh, do I envy you," she said, after a moment of reflection. "Once upon a time . . ." Varvara Petrovna sighed. "In any case, you will not leave me," she concluded. "You're happy here; you're free. You come and go at whatever time you like. What more do you want? I won't be separated from you."

There was something pathetic in that final sentence, and

Ariane felt it. She tried in vain to sway her aunt. Varvara would hear none of it.

The truth is that via a long road she had arrived at a strange state of mind. She hadn't failed to note that Vladimir Ivanovich always came when Ariane was home; that he took pleasure in her niece's brilliant conversation; that he sought out occasions to run into her. At first, she had been silently irritated by this, but she soon understood that Ariane's presence was a sure means of attracting her flighty lover, and that if the girl vanished, Vladimir's appearances would grow increasingly rare. She had reached a point where seeing—just seeing—Vladimir Ivanovich was the only thing that mattered to her. And so she said to herself, "What am I risking? Ariane is a child; for her the doctor is nearly an old man. She's courted by handsome young men in their twenties and thirties. It's from among them that she'll take a lover. Vladimir doesn't interest her. In order to understand how exceptional he is, you have to know life, like I do."

Poor Varvara saw no farther than that. She held on to Ariane in order to hold on to Vladimir, not considering the dangerous game she was playing.

As a result, Ariane ran aground when she told her aunt that she had to go to the university.

At the end of the conversation Ariane looked her aunt in the eye and simply said to her, "That's fine. You're the one who wanted it," and left a worried Varvara to reflect on the meaning of these enigmatic words.

The same evening, Ariane, after assuring herself that no one was around to hear her, went to the telephone in the dining room, asked for a number, and spoke a short phrase into it.

A month passed. We were in the heart of a hot and stormy summer when an incident occurred in the house on the Dvoranskaya. One day, around eight o'clock, as Varvara was returning from a drive in her coach, she found the door of her apartment open and so didn't have to ring. Her step was lively and light and she crossed the dining room without being heard by anyone. The door to Ariane's room was open, and deep in the room she saw the young girl, wearing a filmy white dress, leaning against the wall. In front of her, his two hands on the partition, imprisoning her, Vladimir Ivanovich was leaning in so closely that it seemed to Varvara that her lover's face was touching that of her niece.

She had enough strength to head to her own part of the house without a sound. She rang the bell and the entire household soon learned that Varvara Petrovna was ill. Everyone bustled around her.

The next day, she summoned Ariane and said in a detached tone, "I've changed my mind. I have no right to keep you here. You should make your life as you see fit and study if that makes you happy. So go to the university, in Moscow, in Petersburg, in Liège, or wherever the devil you want. I'll provide you with the means to live. With two hundred rubles, you'll be a rich student; you'll have beautiful dresses, fine linens, and perfumes from Paris."

Ariane's response stunned her aunt. "In fact, I will go to the university," she said. "I decided to long ago. But I don't need money. Thank you, but I've made arrangements. I am and always will be free."

Varvara tried in vain to make her niece speak. Her curiosity was piqued. But she was unable to get anything out of her. Ariane left without clarifying matters.

Once she was alone, Varvara had the unpleasant feeling

that she knew nothing about her niece, whom she'd seen born and who had been with her for three years. In this young girl, apparently so open and easy, there was something dark whose mystery she was unable to pierce. For the first time Varvara understood that she had no hold on Ariane. Her niece was escaping her. Who was she?

Deeply upset, she wasn't keen on speaking to Vladimir Ivanovich about any of this that evening, or on expressing her concern. He shared her fears. Overwhelmed by the emotion that had them both in its grasp, Vladimir was unable to hide from his mistress that he loved Ariane Nicolaevna madly. The scene was strange and touching. The two lovers mingled their tears; it had been a long time since they'd shared so intimate a moment.

In the middle of the summer unpleasant rumors about Ariane Nicolaevna began to spread around town. Twice, regulars at the Hôtel de Londres asserted they'd seen her walking the corridors late at night. One of them said that after midnight she had entered a room "where champagne was drunk." The other said he'd run into her alone, late one night, descending the grand staircase of the hotel. One can imagine how the rumormongers feasted on this! To be sure, Ariane Nicolaevna was not the first person who was rumored to have lovers, and people had grown used to seeing extreme liberty in the attitude of young girls. But everything has its limit. That a young girl should have a flirtation and go beyond that word—well, what Russian would be surprised at this or express condemnation? There's never any problem finding explanations, if not excuses, and only fools pretend to be surprised. But the parties, the suppers at the Hôtel de Londres, the inevitable publicity: that was where scandal began. Ariane Nicolaevna was not spared. Girls and women had no great love for her. She had too many successes, and notable ones at that. Almost every man who came near her fell for her. She was a dangerous rival, and Ariane apparently had no interest in conciliating women. There was in her a mix of haughtiness and mockery that, truth be told, caused her to be hated. She took pleasure in ruining the best-established unions, in destroying happy couples, legitimate or not. And that summer it seemed that the devil had taken possession of her and that she had determined to avenge herself—though no one knew for what—by turning men's heads, preferably those involved in notorious relationships. What she gave them, no one knew, but people assumed the worst. And the sheer number of lovers she was supposed to have left no room for indulgence.

Regretfully, it must be added that a more precisely outlined scandal broke out in which her name was mentioned. One evening around eleven o'clock, two bons vivants who had eaten and drunk more than was advisable decided, accompanied by some women, to go to the small house on the outskirts of town owned by Leon, the concierge at the Hôtel de Londres. They knew it well, having more than once in the past enjoyed the discreet hospitality it offered people desiring to hide their good fortune. They didn't know that since early summer the house had been rented to the engineer Michel Ivanovich Bogdanov.

They reached the house by coach and rang the bell. No one answered. Angered by this silence, they began to knock on the door. It finally opened and they found themselves before the old servant, who declared that the house was rented by Bogdanov and that they should leave without causing a scandal. She wasn't able to convince them; they didn't grasp what she said and were determined to enter and drink. The old woman shouted. They pushed her aside, and despite the women, who tried to hold them back, began to climb the staircase. Michel Ivanovich appeared in the corridor, cane in hand, and ordered them to leave. They pushed him away. He was able to escape into a room, from which he called the police. Upon which a door opened along the corridor and a young woman, her face half-covered by a scarf, escaped at a run and made it onto the street. The two women, who'd remained in the coach and had hesitated before continuing on their way, thought they saw the delicate and elegant Ariane Nicolaevna, known by all in town.

The next day the whole town knew about it. A thousand details were added. The young girl had been surprised in Bogdanov's bed; she had fled in a nightshirt; one of the two women had lent her her coat. Others said that she'd fainted, that the police had called in a doctor, et cetera, et cetera. Every one of these facts was presented as absolutely true by people certain of what they were asserting.

The scandal was enormous. Ariane Nicolaevna continued to stroll about town, to go to the Alexander Garden, to sup with her friends as if these rumors had nothing to do with her. Even so, a week later she spent ten days in the countryside on her aunt's property.

I forgot to note that before this latest scene she had the man who called himself her fiancé to her home. She conversed with him at length and announced her departure for the university. Nicolas had not been unaware of the thousands of remarks circulating the city about Ariane Nicolaevna. There's no need to say that he hadn't believed a single word of what was told him. The look he gave people who spoke in this way caused them to quickly go silent and change the subject.

He received what Ariane told him without surprise, seeming to have foreseen it. He suffered no crisis of despair, but in the calmest, most assured tone he explained to her that he understood her decision; that she had the right to work two or three more years; but that he didn't renounce her: he would wait for her and in the end they would be husband and wife, for that was the only way things could be. "It is written in heaven" were the words he used.

After this conversation he didn't show himself in town and didn't leave his country property.

September arrived and Ariane was ready to depart. At the station, on the evening of her departure, a strange scene occurred. She was there with Varvara Petrovna, Dr. Vladimir Ivanovich, Olga Dimitrievna, and a few of her young friends. She embraced her aunt at the door of the train car. Suddenly a kind of colossus bulled his way through the group. Nicolas Ivanov, for that's who it was, shoved Ariane into the coupé where Olga Dimitrievna was seated. He was paler than usual and looked to be out of control. He rose up before the girl, looked at her briefly, and then punched her, throwing her onto the banquette. Nicolas trembled, fell to his knees, and, seizing Ariane's skirt, kissed the hem again and again. He stood up and, leaving his hat, which had fallen off, on the ground, fled into the night.

The bell struck for the third time, and the train whistled and pulled out before the stunned witnesses to the attack.

PART TWO

1. BORIS GODUNOV

THAT EVENING—it was now April—Chaliapin appeared for the first time that season at Moscow's Bolshoi Theater in the role of Boris Godunov. Nothing equaled the brilliance of the hall, where all the seats had been reserved three weeks in advance. The braided uniforms of the officers and functionaries, the gleam of their decorations, the bright colors of the ribbons, the luminous outfits of the women, the shimmer of the pearls, and the sparkling of the diamonds composed an ensemble rich in color and splendor.

Ariane Nicolaevna was seated in the fourth row of the orchestra. Even though it was already seven o'clock, the seat next to hers was still empty. Ariane looked at her neighbors indifferently and from time to time consulted the program, which she crumpled in her bare hands. She turned and raised her eyes towards the second gallery. It was with some difficulty that she made out a tiny white speck among a thousand similar specks: the clean-shaven face of a student in gold epaulets. The student's face was turned towards hers. She gave him a friendly nod, to which he at length responded.

The orchestra began to play. The seat alongside her remained empty.

Ariane was in a bad mood, a bad mood that had lasted weeks. Her six months in Moscow had not brought the enchantments she'd promised herself they would. She'd felt isolated, lost in an immense city. At home she was queen; the world was at her feet. Here she'd had to start from scratch. Ariane would have had the strength to do so, but a disagreeable experience had disgusted her with the undertaking. In her solitude and her boredom with family life—for she lived (her final concession to her father) at the home of a married uncle with whom she didn't get along, no more than she did with his wife—she frequented the theaters, in particular the admirable Art Theater. She had fallen for one of the leading actors of this unique company, had followed his repertory, and finally had gotten to know him. He had taken her for drives in his automobile; they'd dined in restaurants and in his home. And then suddenly, after a few months of intimacy, she had realized his mediocrity and left him without saying a word, in the most scornful fashion. The adventure had left a bitter aftertaste. She'd tried to work. Her professors had disappointed her. In short, she was angry with Moscow for the disillusionment she'd experienced there.

Onstage, the common folk outside the gate of the monastery implored the unseen Boris to accept the crown and to put an end to their suffering. The sadness of their alternating chants rent the soul.

At just that moment a young man entered the row in which Ariane was sitting, passed in front of the girl, excusing himself, and sat in the empty seat. Ariane saw that he was tall, of unknown age, with something casual and self-assured in the way he carried himself. A few minutes passed and her neighbor, whose gaze she had felt weighing on her several times, asked her in a whisper, "Who's singing Boris this evening?"

She turned towards him a face whose astonishment she made no effort to hide. "Chaliapin, naturally."

The neighbor gestured, as if to say that now he understood how surprising his question was, smiled, and said, "I'll explain during the intermission."

Ariane suppressed the desire to laugh that came over her, and remained silent.

The curtain fell on the end of the first tableau and the hall was illuminated.

The neighbor continued, "What must you think of me? And yet my ignorance can be explained. I arrived in Moscow only today. As I was heading for the Hotel National at seven, I learned by chance that *Boris Godunov* was being performed and I rushed here."

"But you didn't have a seat," Ariane said, interested despite herself.

"Oh," he said, with a smile, "you should know that wherever I go, there's always a seat for me. The cashier turned me away, it's true, but in the lobby an old woman, who was probably waiting for me, offered me the ticket of someone who had fallen ill. See how simple it is?"

"Indeed."

The curtain rising on Boris's entry put a halt to a conversation that both were enjoying.

During the intermission there was great commotion in the hall. Ariane's neighbor said to her, "I'm dying of hunger. Please do me the honor of joining me at the buffet, for I feel I can't part from you."

"I'm not alone," she said. "I was accompanied by a student. He waited in line twenty-four hours to get tickets, one in the amphitheater, the other here."

"One more reason for us to leave."

Ariane Nicolaevna followed him.

During the performance they made so much progress in

their acquaintance that during the final intermission he offered to take her home. She objected that the student had ordered an automobile for her. And then, having second thoughts, she said, "Actually, that will be an excellent lesson."

And hardly had the curtain come down than they ran like two children at the end of the school day. He proposed a supper. Absolutely no way. He wanted to take a coach. She opposed it. She was determined to return on foot, even though she lived in the Sadovaya, a half hour from the center of town. So there they were, stumbling through the mud and melted snow. The holes in the pavement and the uncertainty of the obstacles on the road legitimized the offer—one not refused—of an arm. He looked at her as he spoke. She was wearing a black cape over her elegant and low-cut evening attire and, on her head, an astounding small soft felt hat that she had pulled, crumpled, from one of her coat pockets. They were already making plans for the future.

"Since you love music," he said, "please agree to come see *Prince Igor* with me the day after tomorrow."

"But you won't have seats."

He stopped, stood before her, and took her two hands.

"Don't you know that I always get what I want? So we'll hear *Prince Igor*, and since this time we'll be old acquaintances, you won't refuse to dine with me."

"Fine. If you can get us seats I agree. But it's sold out."

They had arrived at a beautiful apartment building in the Sadovaya.

"Here's my house."

"Speaking of which, give me your name and phone number."

He wrote as she dictated and then offered her his card.

She read: "Constantin Michel."
"That's not a name," she said.
"And yet it's mine."

2. A SUPPER

One could find, from the beginning of a relationship,
a few moments in which to speak reasonably.
—Étienne Pivert de Senancour, *De l'Amour*

TWO DAYS later, Constantin Michel and Ariane Nicolaevna were seated alongside each other on a sofa in a private
room in the Hermitage's famous restaurant. Ariane was in
a very good mood. Constantin let her tell her story, taking
the greatest pleasure in the tales she narrated. He already
knew Varvara Petrovna, and he knew that the girl had a
sort-of-fiancé, Nicolas Ivanov, who, even before the wedding,
had suffered some bitter experiences. He wasn't unaware of
either the suppers in the Hôtel de Londres or the court of
admirers who surrounded the brilliant Ariane Nicolaevna
there. He thought the Alexander Garden to be the most
seductive public garden in Russia, where a thousand intrigues
were hatched and undone amidst contrasting dark alleys
and terraces shimmering beneath the glow of electric globes.
With just a few sharp strokes Ariane Nicolaevna had been
able to evoke the framework and the main characters of her
past life. It was as if he saw before him Varvara Petrovna's
light step, her irresistible smile. Poor Nicolas cut a sorry
figure in this tableau. A number of personalities filed through
the shadowy darkness, about whom Ariane, who generally
took pride in speaking her mind, said almost nothing, leav-

ing it to her companion's sagacity to guess her thoughts from her hinds.

As amused as he was, Constantin Michel was even more perplexed. Who was this imperious, willful, witty, intelligent young girl? She knew life like a woman. At times there was something serious in her gaze. Her brow was determined and thoughtful. And yet the other evening, when she'd put on her cape and the bizarre little black hat that she wore at the university, she looked like a sixteen-year-old girl. "She's from the south, it's true," he said to himself, "but however precocious girls there might be, several years of experience are needed to accumulate the storehouse of practical knowledge she's trying to display for my benefit."

He stopped in the middle of his reflections and abruptly asked, "Speaking of which, how old are you?"

"Speaking of what?" she said, surprised by his words, which in no way responded to what she had been saying at the moment.

He explained himself. "When I look at you, you're seventeen. When I listen to you, you're thirty, and a well-employed thirty years. So I don't understand—"

She cut him off. "Is it necessary to understand a woman? One takes her. That's the shortest route."

He gave a start and was dumbfounded for a second. And then, speaking in the tone set by Ariane Nicolaevna's sharp remark, he told her of his uncertainty as to her age from the moment he'd met her, and that she seemed to him at times to be a child and at others like a young woman who'd been around.

Her lips were curled ironically, and when he finished speaking she tossed off, with the tone of a theater lover applauding a showy effect, "Not bad."

"But your answer?" he said. "Depending on the hour, I bet even money on seventeen and twenty-five."

"As always," she said, "the truth lies in the middle."

And the conversation veered off into another direction.

A short while later, after they'd finished eating, and as the refrain of the gypsy tunes played by a nearby orchestra filtered through the partition of the private room, Constantin Michel leaned towards the young girl, put his arm around her supple waist, and drew her to him. She didn't resist, but as his lips approached hers she turned her head and they fell upon Ariane Nicolaevna's cool neck, at the base of her ear, near her hair.

She remained in his arms, motionless, and it was he who pulled away an instant later, saying, "What perfume do you use? It's delicious."

Ariane looked surprised and responded simply, "That, too, is my secret."

A silence fell.

Constantin broke it deliberately. He had made a decision, and in a tone that contrasted with that of the conversation until then, he told the girl that he had an excessive love of honesty, that a clear and simple way of saying things had always served him well, and that he would attempt it one more time, even if it were to cost him dearly. At the very least he was certain that with the intelligence he knew she possessed, she wouldn't misunderstand him; perhaps she'd even be grateful to him.

"The truth," he continued, "is that I want to win you. I admit this with no beating around the bush. How can I succeed in this? Will I employ with you, Ariane Nicolaevna, the means men usually use when they want to seduce a woman? Will I let you believe that you are the first woman before whom I have knelt? You'd laugh in my face. Let's speak plainly. You please me infinitely. You perhaps find me agreeable, since you are here. At your side I don't imagine I will know the boredom that is, after all, our only—but mortal —enemy. So I want to see you more, and better, and every day..."

He stopped. Ariane said nothing. Slightly embarrassed, he said, "Help me, Ariane Nicolaevna! I'm not used to giving speeches."

"I'm waiting for the end foretold by so beautiful a beginning."

"In that case, I'll continue. Have you read Heinrich Heine's *Reisebilder*?"

She shook her head no. She looked distracted.

Constantin continued: "In the *Reisebilder*, Heine recounts that one day he arrives in a village where he is to pass the night. He sees a beautiful girl in a window watering flowers, and says to her, more or less, 'I wasn't here yesterday, I'll no longer be here tomorrow, but today is ours.' And the girl offers him a flower... I will only be in Moscow a short time, but I propose that we spend this short time together. I'm not free, Ariane Nicolaevna. I'll leave one day and won't return. Life is a gloomy affair. You need ingenuity, will, and savoir faire to get from it—I won't say happiness—but at least pleasure. Would you like us to form a precarious association in pursuit of pleasure? I feel I can speak to you in this way and that you will perhaps appreciate the oddity and boldness of a proposal I wouldn't dare address in this fashion to anyone but you. But you are lacking in hypocrisy and you look matters square in the face; I'm convinced of this. What do we risk? Understand me without my spelling things out: we risk nothing. Forgive me, but I'm forgetting a great danger. Perhaps you'll fall in love with me, or I with you. Love, which is outside our agreement, will perhaps slip in. Are we going to retreat before this imaginary danger? You are brave, and I'm not lacking in that quality. I rush headlong at the foe…"

He took the young girl in his arms. She didn't resist, and, leaning over her, he said, "Forgive me, Ariane Nicolaevna, but I'm at a moment when falsehood is odious to me. Whatever happens, we won't have misled each other."

She was going to respond when he closed her mouth with a kiss and added, "Don't speak, please."

She pulled herself free, stretched, took a purple carnation from her corsage, put it to her lips, and then carelessly tossed it into the corner.

"I once heard," she said, "of people who wanted to achieve the same ends as you. They went about it differently…We never stop learning, no matter our age. But it's late and tonight's lesson has gone on long enough. I'm going home. Speaking of which, have I told you that the uncle who's putting me up has fallen for me? I'm going to have to lock myself in, and it's strange, but I suffocate in a room with a closed door."

They departed in a coach. As he was leaving Ariane Nicolaevna he said to her, "See you tomorrow. Would you like to dine with me?"

"No, I'm dining here at seven."

"Fine. I'll wait for you at your door at half past eight and you will be kind enough to take tea in my apartment."

"Absolutely not!"

3. AN ORDINARY SOIREE

THE NEXT evening at half past eight Ariane appeared at the door of her house, where Constantin Michel was waiting for her. She was wearing a ravishing broad-brimmed hat, with ribbons tied below her chin. Her bare neck stood out from her cape.

They went down the Tverskaya. It was understood that they'd "take a stroll." Even so, having reached the National Hotel, Constantin proposed that they go inside.

"Why not?" she said.

And beneath the heavy coat a frail shoulder rose and communicated a slight movement to the thick fabric.

In the small sitting room Ariane took off her coat and then, going into the bedroom, took off her hat and fixed her hair before the mirror. She looked around her, displaying no sign of embarrassment. On the bed, prepared in anticipation of the night, Constantin's pajamas were laid out.

They drank tea in the sitting room. Constantin sat the young girl on his lap and their mouths met. He began to undress her. At this point Ariane put up a stubborn resistance, her sharp nails playing a role in the combat. It required will and strength, cajolery and strong reinforcements of ingenuity and ruses to conquer, one by one, each article of clothing. The light blouse fell, the firm, round young breasts appeared on a skinny chest. It took an eternity to get off the skirt, but

Constantin finally succeeded. He held the almost-naked girl in his arms.

His agitation was at its height. Civilization has taught women to put up only a simulacrum of resistance in circumstances like these, just enough so that he can carry out the action of ancient conquest. It's a charming comedy whose scenes have long since been established. But in this case, contrary to the agreement tacitly reached with Ariane, he was forced to fight and use force. Why was she so bitterly defending herself, since she had decided to give herself? Why had she fought for an hour without respite? During a brief truce he couldn't help brutally saying to her, "Come now, you know why we're here. You're a girl who knows what's what. After all, it's not your first time..."

Ariane looked at him with the air of a goddess and said in a tone that made Constantin feel the absurdity of his question, "You can't possibly have imagined that I waited for you, did you?"

Her shoulder rose and came out of the blouse, which slid along her arm, leaving half her torso nude. But when Constantin tried to carry the girl to the bedroom, she clung to the sofa and said in a clear voice, "I have some conditions."

"I accept them in advance," the exasperated Constantin answered.

"There'll be no light and I'll lie here as if I were dead."

Constantin Michel reflected. "Who in God's name am I involved with? Here I am, embarked on an adventure with one of those unhinged girls of today who make love as easily as they eat, with no meaning or appetite. They give neither the one nor the other any importance. Let's hope I don't regret it."

The girl's fresh young body girl was in his arms, and he

responded, "Those conditions are absurd, but now is not the moment to discuss them ..."

In the night of the room, in the warmth of the sheets where Ariane was "lying like a dead woman," he saw from an obvious—though involuntary—sign that at least the first of the two suppositions that had just occurred to him had no basis. Meanwhile, the fight continued in the darkness, the fight with the corpse.

Irritated, he sharply told her, "There are times when it's fine to fight. There are others when one must know when to give oneself."

"But I'm not fighting," a voice in his ear said, a small voice, a humble, childish voice, through which there seemed to pass a breath of fright, and whose new timbre struck him.

And at that very moment, he emerged triumphant.

An hour later, seated before the dressing table, she straightened her long, luxurious hair. It reached the curve of her hips, and its undulating waves hid her frail torso.

She spoke detachedly and freely, telling stories from her past. There wasn't a word, not a gaze, that testified to the novelty of the relations that had just been established between them. As he listened to her, Constantin noticed a thin cut on one of the fingers of his right hand. "That little monster scratched me," he thought, "or perhaps it was a pin."

As midnight tolled she rose. He hoped in vain to take her out for supper.

"My lover is waiting for me at home," she said. "He made a scene yesterday evening: it seems he guessed where I was coming from. My aunt heard him, and there was a second scene. I want to avoid another one: I like having peace in my home."

They returned on foot. She spoke volubly of the programs

at the gymnasium and the education of girls. When he left her at her door she seemed surprised to hear Constantin ask if he could see her the next day at the same time. She accepted with no discussion.

Back home, as he repaired the disorder of the bed before going to sleep, he saw a few drops of blood on the sheet. "She scratched me more deeply than I thought. What a strange little beast! What were my predecessors like? I have to start her education over again. But is it worth the trouble?"

He was tired and, giving no more thought to the matter, fell asleep.

4. SURGIT AMARI ALIQUID

THEIR life settled into a routine. Constantin never saw Ariane during the day, which she spent at the university. He occupied himself with his affairs, which were important. He lunched once with his official mistress, Baroness Korting, the most beautiful woman in Moscow, who was surprised by his lack of eagerness. He struggled to come up with excuses.

But every evening at half past eight in the Sadovaya, he met his student in her cape. Every evening they walked to the National Hotel; every evening they went to bed in a hot, dark room, and, when midnight tolled, got dressed and repeated the walk in reverse, talking the whole way, animatedly and with mutual pleasure.

She had clear opinions on every subject, which she expressed with such certainty that they allowed for no contradiction. She constructed systems of the most extreme materialism, leaving no place for feelings, mercilessly mocking pity and love. Occasionally he amused himself by destroying with a word the marvelous castles she so nobly built in the air, but more often than not he allowed her fantasies to run free. She roamed as if drunk through the world of ideas, while he never ceased to admire the gushing, clear force of her thoughts. Constantin Michel knew the world, London, New York, Rome, Paris... "With just a touch of polish," he thought, "with that elegance of form that one only learns in the West, with the tone and the vocabulary of the high society over there, is there a single capital in the universe where, after a short training period and an indispensable adjustment, that little Russian girl would not triumph? The finest of minds would delight in her."

He couldn't imagine a more attractive companion. She incited him to think and kept him in a feverish state of endlessly renewed ideas and sensations.

He sensed in her the inexhaustible riches of the Russian nature, the gift, the generosity, and the lavish giving of the self that compose it. "All she is lacking to reach the greatest heights is either a method or the presence of a superior man. But it must be admitted," he concluded, "that the men around here are not up to the task."

Every day Constantin Michel waited impatiently for the hours that brought Ariane back to him. He compared her to Baroness Korting, who was more beautiful than she, who was good, kind, and agreeable, but who, from having lived too long in the West, had taken on the artificiality that reigns in the sitting rooms of France and England. There was nothing he could hold against her, except the most important thing in the world: she bored him.

Boredom was unknown to those around Ariane. It wasn't even possible to conceive of it, so changeable, amusing, gay, serious, contradictory, capricious, difficult, and touchy was she, imprisoned in her self-esteem as if in an impregnable fortress.

When she was at his home for dinner it was an especial delight. A supper—which was rarer—took on the appearance of a feast. The long strolls between the Sadovaya and the National Hotel seemed to them too short. They would linger, talking into the night, and, having arrived at the doorway, prolonged the conversation even further.

But in the apartment in the National Hotel another Ariane appeared. He had before him a woman who remained a stranger to him. From the day he had had her, he had thought that the natural relations between lover and mistress would be established between them. He now recognized his error. He thought he'd conquered her, and the conquest was constantly called into question. He felt he'd made no progress. His mistress belonged to him only through a fiction. In reality, she was elusive: she escaped him. He kissed her and she allowed herself to be kissed and took pleasure in it. But she never came to him on her own, in a spontaneous, tender impulse.

He remarked on this to her one day. The response he received sent a chill down his spine. "Don't pay any attention to it," she said. "I'm always like this."

"What a terrible education she's had," Constantin Michel thought. "What fools did she know before me?"

In bed she continued to play the dead woman. And yet Constantin sometimes felt the involuntary pressure of an arm pulling him to her. Only once did she go so far as to complain of having to get up, confessing that she was exhausted. It took her a week to admit that the bedroom door was open onto the sitting room, where the lights were still on. And yet she didn't use modesty as an excuse. She got out of bed, went to the bathroom, and returned naked to fix her hair in front of the mirror with the calm assurance of a well-built young girl with nothing to hide.

Each encounter was thus a combat between the man's ardor and the woman's coldness. What was irritating was that Constantin felt that this coldness was calculated, commanded by an effort of will. He never forced Ariane into his bed: she came there of her own free volition, but when she lay in the sheets she seemed to die inside. She, who upright could not be quiet, remained silent, her eyes open. During the first week of their liaison, the best he was able to get out of her, as he whispered in her ear the eternal words lovers tell the women they possess, was an ambiguous *nichevo*.

Outside they spoke freely, like two friends. In bed he found the enemy, one who had always to be vanquished and who never admitted defeat.

This combat excited Constantin Michel, and he swore to emerge from it victorious. Nevertheless, he was deeply wounded by Ariane's attitude, from which she never wavered.

But these were only skirmishes.

On the fourth or fifth evening, as she was getting dressed and he was smoking a cigarette while seated at the foot of the bed, he asked offhandedly two of those banal questions that men ask a mistress who was just in their arms.

She didn't answer. He repeated his phrase.

Without raising her head towards him, without stopping to free herself from his arms, she responded nonchalantly, as if she didn't feel the venom in her response, "I'm waiting for the third question, the one all the men who've had me asked after the two you just asked."

Constantin Michel blanched. He had the strength to control himself, to not add a word. He finished his cigarette, went into the bathroom, and stayed there longer than usual. When he came out, midnight had chimed. "Let's go," he said.

She moved closer to him, leaned on his arm, and asked, "What's wrong with you today? You look sad. I'm not the reason for it, am I?"

"Nothing, my little one, nothing. You're delicious, as

always." He was now addressing her in the familiar form, while she continued to use the formal one.

Along the way they argued over a philosophical point, both defending their position violently, almost bitterly. Finally, Constantin Michel broke out in laughter. "Where the devil do we find things to quarrel about?"

And he embraced Ariane, who continued to defend herself.

The following evening the struggle resumed, but in a more guarded fashion, the adversaries striving not to reveal themselves.

Constantin wanted to know why Ariane Nicolaevna, who had her options and had exercised them more than once, had taken him, Constantin Michel, and had given herself at their third meeting. He didn't imagine that he was irresistible, and Ariane didn't love him. But whatever liberty a girl might grant herself, it is difficult to accept that she will go so far as to take a lover the same way a man chooses a mistress, often for no longer than an hour. Why was she there with him? In a roundabout way, he sought clarification on this point.

He spoke of the famous *Boris Godunov* evening and returned to his first impression of her, his long hesitation between "young woman" and "child."

"And you," he said, "what did you think of me? After all, it's the first impression that commands all the rest."

"Me," she said, "I told myself, 'He fits the pattern,' for I have to admit that in my experience only blond men have character. Brown-haired men make an impression, but it quickly burns out. You take them and nothing is left in your hands. The wise thing to do, after a few unhappy experiences, is to return to what has worked out."

She chatted away agreeably, as if she were talking about the weather on this day in May.

Constantin Michel felt like he'd swallowed a bitter drug. He felt that the only way to respond to a provocation of this kind was with blows. But he had to win the battle and, in the first instance, gain time. He took out a cigarette, lit it, and with an easy, kind smile affectionately scolded, "Ariane, Ariane . . . These are things one thinks but doesn't say. You're nothing but a little Cossack."

"But I hate lying," she said. "It's too difficult, so I say things as they occur to me. You must have noticed this . . . Admit it, I'm lacking in delicacy and guile. The way I act with you has proved this. Are you angry with me?"

He didn't have the strength to take her in his arms and kiss her lips, as it would have been politic to do. He still had a bitter aftertaste in his mouth that wasn't going to disappear quickly. He limited himself to a few warm and banal protests. "In truth," he said "you attract me because you're yourself. There are a few drawbacks that go along with this, but there are more advantages to it than disadvantages. Obviously, you express with simplicity things that a Western woman would die rather than admit. Should I confess that once the initial surprise has passed, this harsh honesty has its price? Perhaps I'll end up finding a perverse pleasure in it."

But that same evening, returning on foot from the Sadovaya at around one o'clock, Constantin clenched his fists and exhaled his rage. He felt attacked, scorned by that little girl, who, while looking as if butter wouldn't melt in her mouth, had injured him where it hurt, keeping the wound open every day and poisoning it with a knowing art. For whatever the degree of honesty one allows oneself, love, even physical love, must be draped in illusions. Illuminating it brutally and in that way sets it to fleeing. One must drive from one's thoughts the idea that in the arms of a woman one encounters the more or less effaced shades of one's predecessors. These are things one doesn't think of when one is healthy of mind, unless one is madly in love. Yet Constantin Michel claimed that he was healthy of mind and not in love. To be sure, he was attached to Ariane, and in more ways than one. She had the taste of a delicious ripe fruit, whose occasional acidity sets one's teeth on edge. But it was never a question of love, and so it was easy to forget Ariane's past.

And now this demon of a girl constantly waved it in front of his face and forced him to confront it. At first, he thought she acted this way out of clumsiness, out of a lack of instinct that, oddly, is often found among the most intelligent women. In this there was perhaps an error in education. Aunt Varvara, who spoke so freely to her niece, must have been responsible, not to mention this Russian provincial environment... It would suffice to warn Ariane Nicolaevna.

But Constantin quickly recognized his error. No, it wasn't by chance that she spoke in this way. He divined in her a thought-out plan, a premeditated and long-term offensive. His unfailing instincts told him that Ariane knew exactly where to wound him, and that she maintained her hold on him.

And yet it was impossible to allow her to continue this way, at risk of being poisoned.

At this point in his reflections Constantin Michel reversed himself. "When it comes down to it, what am I bothering myself about? I have a deliciously young girl in my arms every evening and the most amusing conversation partner I've ever met. In a month or six weeks I'll have left Russia and we'll never see each other again. Let's just let things run their course."

This is how he spoke, but they were nothing but words, for deep down he still tasted the bitter poison Ariane had distilled and poured into him. Since it amused him to try to see things clearly, he said to himself, "Why do I lend so much importance to that girl's past? Perhaps I'm more attached to her than I think. What folly it would be to fall in love with a girl with a checkered past who fell into my arms without offering the least resistance—who would have fallen into the neighbor's arms if I hadn't been there! She is rich in youth and intelligence, but she has a defect that will in the long run make her unbearable to me: she's wicked. She already knows how to make me suffer, but she can only get away with using that detestable science as long as I allow her to. I'm free. The day I'm tired of her, I'll take my leave. For the moment, only the desire to vanquish the coldness she affects ties me to her. That, and nothing more."

He dreamt of the near future. Where would he be in a month? In Constantinople or New York, in any case far from Ariane Nicolaevna. He had work to do. And wherever he went, he would meet other women. Life is infinite. How ridiculous to think of imprisoning it beneath the black cape of a little student at Moscow University.

Constantin Michel walked quickly. He was in a good mood when he reached the National Hotel and had a light supper before going to his room. When he entered his bedroom, there still reigned a faint but penetrating scent, the one he'd breathed in a few hours before on Ariane Nicolaevna's neck. The bed was unmade. It seemed as if a gust of sensuality rose from the gaping sheets, which still held the warmth of their two bodies. He had an irresistible urge to squeeze Ariane in his arms, to speak to her harshly, to tell her that he was the master, that he would never again accept her insolence, and to then take her, to caress her endlessly, and spend a night, an entire night, at her side; to fall asleep touching her, to awaken with that young body resting on his. And perhaps then he would again hear that voice, that humble, childlike voice that had sounded in his ear only once, but which he couldn't get out of his mind, and which he sought to find in Ariane's mouth, and which, without admitting it to himself, he awaited every day like a promised miracle, the voice that had said the first night, "But I'm not resisting."

Constantin Michel remained seated on the bed. Suddenly he bounded out of it. "I'm going mad! I'm going to show you that I'm free, little Ariane from nowhere!"

He ran to the telephone and asked for Baroness Korting's number. Despite the lateness of the hour, she wasn't yet in bed. Constantin Michel informed that charming woman that he finally had some free time and asked her if she'd be kind enough to dine with him the next day. Baroness Korting didn't hide the pleasure she felt in accepting the invitation.

The following day at eight o'clock, while Ariane was at her home, he called her on the phone, told her that he had a business dinner that couldn't be put off, that he was sorry he couldn't see her, but that he counted on her for the following day, as usual.

She responded simply, "All right, see you tomorrow." And hung up the phone.

5. BARONESS KORTING

An hour later he dined with Baroness Korting, whom he'd known for several years. She was a woman with whom it was flattering for any man to be seen, for she was beautiful, one of those indisputable beauties who make even little boys turn their heads. And she was good. Constantin had never heard her utter a bad word about anyone. She didn't lack subtlety in matters of love, where the simplest woman understands more and sees more clearly than any man. Finally, she placed Constantin Michel on a pedestal, and she told anyone willing to listen that he was "incomparable."

As a result, Constantin had remained attached to her. She seemed to be the only fixed thing in the nomadic life he lived. One winter he spent a month with her in Nice. Another time, part of a spring in Paris. Twice he'd met her in Moscow, to which he'd gone for business.

He wanted to take her to a restaurant, but she called to ask him to dine at her home. There he once again found a well-arranged house, an elegant and immaculate table, and his eyes looked admiringly on Baroness Korting, dressed in a stylish low-cut dress from rue de la Paix. She received him warmly, spoiled him, pampered him, catered to him, enveloped him in the clouds of incense that usually billowed around her god. She asked him for the latest stories from London and Paris; she told him the latest scandals from

Petersburg and Moscow. Where was he? Everywhere and nowhere, no more in Russia than anywhere else. The maître d'hôtel was Italian, and Baroness Korting was polished with a Western varnish. Why, at the moment he asked himself that question, did he think of the pale little girl of the Sadovaya? That one was truly from his country, despite her European culture. He chased away these thoughts.

Baroness Korting—"Olga" to her close friends—brought him back by asking him what he did with his evenings. No one saw him anywhere. He excused himself, saying he had meetings with businessmen who were busy during the day. Olga, with feminine logic, said to him, "Well then, arrange things so you can have tea at my home. You know I'll always be free at whatever hour you say."

He remained quite late at the home of that kind woman, and the sky was growing light in the east when he crossed the empty streets to return to his hotel. His nerves were calm and his mind at peace. "This is truly wisdom and security," he thought. "The *otium cum dignitate* of the Latins, for, after all, I'm at the mercy of the whims of that fickle girl. I have everything and yet I seek something else. It's absurd. I'm going to liquidate the business on the Sadovaya. I have a trip I need to take to Kiev that's happening at just the right moment to put an end to that adventure, since, when it comes down to it, that's all it is. I'll hasten my departure."

Nevertheless, around seven in the evening, Constantin Michel was surprised to find himself nervous at the thought that Ariane might call and cancel. He was certain that she would do so simply in reprisal for having been abandoned the previous evening. But he had no reason to be nervous. Ariane didn't call, and at half past eight she appeared with her customary punctuality at the door of the Sadovaya.

He was struck by how slender she was, how delicate, the frailty of her entire person. It was only in her brow and in her eyes that one could read strength. He suddenly had a new feeling for her, a strange one for him: that of pity. He felt she was, despite it all, a young girl tossed alone into the dangerous whirlpool of life. She would be crushed by it, as were so many like her who advanced into the tempest, head held high, full of courage, with an air of defiance. And now, at a turn in the road, she had collided with a hard rock—with him, Constantin Michel. He had a fleeting vision of the future. "This story will end badly for you, my child," he thought. "Whatever you might think, you will grow attached to me, and one fine day I'll leave for New York or Shanghai, leaving you alone, lost in the middle of the human sea that is Russia."

He briefly felt an inexpressible emotion. He forgave Ariane her troubled past. She too, though so young, had had an ideal, and not having achieved it, she made those she encountered pay for it.

He passed his arm under that of the girl, pressed her against him, and led her to the hotel. He was nothing but gentleness and gaiety all through the night. Her lover's mood didn't escape Ariane's notice. She allowed herself to be carried along by the irresistible flood of tenderness flowing from Constantin Michel's heart. For the first time she forgot her role, pressed herself against him, snuggled in his arms, and, once she'd gotten out of bed, told the maddest tales of her childhood, an era that held no danger in Constantin's eyes.

It was a brief intermission. A few days later the Machiavellian implacable struggle started up again. One evening, since Ariane was ill and they were having tea in the small sitting room, she began to speak of their relationship. She thanked him for having defined its character with such precision and foresight even before it had begun.

She said, "I appreciate my wise, well-informed friend. Thanks to you, everything is clear between us. There's no room for any ambiguity. I'm free, as are you. We've formed a temporary association in the quest for pleasure, and I won't hide it from you: you've given it to me."

"That's not a small thing," Constantin cut in. "You know Vigny's lines: 'It's pleasure she loves. / Man is brutal and knows how to take but not give it.'"

"I don't know that poem," she said, "but, as is said, I know the song." Constantin Michel was angry with himself for having brought up the quote. "And our chats are no small pleasure. Men are usually so silly. Once we've gotten what we want from them, they go mute."

Constantin began to grimace inside. But how to stop Ariane? He tried to change the subject. With a superior logic, Ariane returned to it. "But since we're free, we have the right to do whatever we want. You can have a mistress" —all right; she knows my story, Constantin thought— "and I can take a lover. We wouldn't be cheating on each other, since we don't love each other and we have given prior notice."

"No, not that! I'm don't believe in sharing," shouted Constantin, who on this subject gave his feelings free rein. "No. A hundred times no! As long as you're mine you belong to no one else. You've been warned."

"And even so, if I had a lover? You'd never know."

"That's where you're wrong. I'd know it, and right away."

"And then..."

"My dear child, to my great regret, it would all be over between us."

He said these words with no anger, but so definitively that it seemed to make an impression on Ariane.

She returned obliquely to this question, which concerned her, a short time later. "But you don't love me."

"That's another question, but as long you belong to me, I'm not surrendering you to anyone."

"You're bizarre," Ariane said.

"I am what I am, and there's nothing to discuss. I've made things clear on this matter, so now let's talk about something else."

With apparent indifference they began to speak about some banal matter.

But when she rose to leave, Constantin was carried away by a sudden impulse. He pushed Ariane against a wall, put his hands on her shoulders, and, looking her straight in the eye, said, "I don't know what game you're playing, little girl. If you want to fight, then let's fight. But I'm warning you that you won't beat me. Rest assured that of the two of us, it's I who will win. And do you want me to tell you what will happen to you? Whether you will it or not, you'll love me. You'll love me with your diabolical mind; with your heart, which is unknown to me; with your body, which I do know."

He felt Ariane's shoulder trying to rise beneath his hand. But he gripped it tightly and the shoulder gave only a hint of the attempted gesture, which, unable to develop, ceased.

6. UNFORESEEN IMPULSE

IN THE meanwhile, Constantin saw Baroness Korting three or four times a week in the afternoon, and Ariane every evening. If he was making any progress with the latter, nothing indicated it. It was already mid-May. Ariane was still exactly the same. One day she was joyful, childish, full of anecdotes and charming expressions. The next day, with an art incomparable in its studied carelessness, she returned to hated subjects, seeming to take pleasure in doing so.

"You don't lie enough," Constantin said to her with a laugh. "You haven't yet understood the secret of happiness, which is based on an illusion dearly nourished and jealously respected."

"There's more than one way to be happy," she responded. "Who knows if mine isn't as good as yours? Can I complain about life?" she added. "Don't I have a handsome and intelligent lover?"

"Ariane, I don't like to be mocked."

"Come now. Since I've chosen you from among so many others without giving myself the time to reflect, it must be that your appearance, your appearance alone, monsieur, has something irresistible about it. To tell you the truth, the student who accompanied me to the theater is quite seductive. But you're better, since I'm here at this hour instead of in his arms. The poor boy. He'd been pursuing me assiduously and respectfully for three months and thought he was about to achieve happiness. The evening at the Bolshoi was to be the decisive one. He'd ordered an automobile! We were going to sup at Jahr's . . ."

Constantin Michel was at his wit's end. To punish himself, like a flagellant who wants to be beaten more, he asked, "What would have happened then?"

"What happens in all these cases, my dear and excellent friend. We would have dined and drunk excellent champagne. Then we'd have returned by automobile—"

"And then?" Constantin asked coldly. "Does he have an apartment? Respectable hotels don't receive people in the middle of the night."

"But there are hotels that aren't respectable," the girl answered. "And from Petrovsky Park to the center of Moscow it's twenty minutes, a route that can be lengthened. A closed automobile, the bumps, the intoxication of the supper, an arm squeezed around the waist, passionate lips on your neck . . . I'm not made of wood, something you know better than anyone."

The following day Constantin decided to leave for Kiev and announced it to Baroness Korting in the afternoon. That evening he told Ariane. She gave a start.

"What? You're leaving on my birthday? That's not nice."

It was the first time she'd demonstrated any sentiment towards him.

He took her in his arms.

"You should have told me, little one," he said. "How could I know? In any case, we'll dine together tomorrow. I'm not leaving till eleven, and only for a week. Speaking of which, how old are you?"

"Eighteen."

"What, eighteen? You led me to believe you were at least twenty."

It was as if she'd misled him on a point of capital importance.

"Eighteen!" he repeated. "Eighteen! That's unimaginable! You can't be eighteen! So when I met you, you were only seventeen! You could have told me that; you should have told me that!"

He was beside himself with exasperation.

She calmed him. "I don't see what our ages have to do with our adventure. I never asked you yours. When we met, a blessed day," she threw out ironically, "I was a month shy of eighteen. What's a month? You're not going to argue with me over one month."

But Constantin Michel hadn't recovered, and the shock produced by what he called a "new fact" had almost immediate unexpected results.

Ariane was telling stories about her aunt Varvara. She commented on the wisdom of that life, its perfect equilibrium, the art with which Varvara Petrovna had been able to pluck only the roses of love.

"Aunt Varvara told me," she continued, "that she never spent the whole night with any of her lovers. You have to know the right moment to leave or ask your lovers to leave. According to her, sleeping together is the surest way to kill love. You sleep badly and you wake up in a bad mood. You're ugly in the light of morning. You should only see your lover when your hair is fixed up and you've neatened yourself. You should only dress and undress to please him. Promiscuity is fine for married couples, but marriage is neither love nor pleasure—"

Constantin cut her off. "Your aunt, with all her experience, doesn't know much about life. However free she might be, she's a woman with a system, and, given what you've just told me, I don't have a high opinion of her. For people who love each other it's not a matter of hours, little one; they separate neither by day nor by night, they lunch and dine at the same table, fall asleep together, and wake up alongside each other. You find it pleasant when we share the same bed and we're so close to each other; when there's nothing either materially or morally between us; when the warmth of our shared bed penetrates us and lulls us; when from the tips of your toes to the top of your head you feel me next to you; when your body adapts itself to mine; when we seem to live just one life, and the beating of your heart joins with mine. Do you find it agreeable to tear yourself from me, to get up, to get dressed? You don't feel the wall that's immediately erected between us and each garment you put on. You again become a stranger; you again become the enemy."

Constantin had become strangely heated, surprising even himself. Ariane clapped her hands and mocked him. "How eloquent you are!"

"It's your aunt's foolishness that irritates me. It's got nothing to do with you or with me. To the devil with her! What ideas she put in your head!"

He paced the room for some time. Ariane was silent.

Suddenly he stopped in front of her. "You know what we're going to do? When do you take your final exam?"

She told him a date a week off.

"Fine," he continued. "I'll be back from Kiev and you'll have finished with the university. You need some fresh air and I want some rest. I've worked a great deal and Moscow has strangely gotten on my nerves. I'll take you to Crimea and we'll spend two weeks in the southern sun, on red rocks at the seaside, among the flowers and under the trees. We'll live like gods. We won't think or argue. This is my *ne varietur* plan. You have only to obey."

Hardly had he finished than he was stunned by what he'd said. What was he throwing himself into? Was this the way he intended to liquidate the adventure he had begun? Clearly, in the irritating contact with Ariane, he had lost his mind.

However, she raised objections, which she calmly stated. Her aunt would be expecting her the day she finished her exams in Moscow. She received three or four letters a week imploring her not to waste an hour. Varvara's relationship with the handsome doctor had turned tragic and Ariane was needed there. Her friends as well, who had their rights, counted on her presence. Finally, another reason, which she alluded to while leaving it unspoken, compelled her to return on a given date.

The more she talked, the more Constantin proved to himself how excellent his plan was. He concluded the discussion by telling her, with the calm assurance he felt held sway over the young girl, "I want to go to Crimea with you. That's all there is to it, and it shall be done. You'll never make me believe that a clever girl like you can't steal the two weeks that we need. I'll leave it up to you and won't give you any advice on the matter. Today is the eighteenth and I return from Kiev on the twenty-eighth. You'll have taken your exam the same day, and on the twenty-ninth we'll take the express train to Sebastopol. You'll reclaim your liberty between June fifteenth and June twentieth."

Having said this, he refused any further discussion, and

the next day he was on the platform of the Kiev station with Ariane, for she hadn't refused to accompany him. For the first time in the six weeks he had known her, he had succeeded in having her accept a gift—in honor of her eighteenth birthday—and a wristwatch encircled the girl's wrist.

"Prepare your valises for the twenty-ninth," he said.

"But I assure you that it's impossible."

The bell sounded. He took Ariane in his arms. It seemed to him that she had never embraced him that way, that she had never given herself to him as completely as in that hurried kiss on the station platform.

He thought about it at length on the train. "Am I wrong? Is it an illusion? No, no, it's the truth. That girl, usually so guarded, gave herself away this time."

7. CRIMEA

CONSTANTIN Michel returned from Kiev a week later. Every evening between five o'clock and seven o'clock, the day over, he awaited the arrival of the night on the terrace of the Merchants' Garden. The view enjoyed from there is one of the most beautiful in the world. To the left, above the terrace, are the heavily populated port quarters. To the right, in the greenery, the white walls and golden cupolas of the Kiev Pechersk monastery, the holiest place in Russia. And then the slow-moving Dnieper, with its long bends, the steamboats furrowing it, the caravans of barges, the rising smoke, the whistles rending the silence. And in the distance, the Russian plain, leading without a wrinkle to the horizon, and the great, dark daub of the forest towards the east. It was a vast landscape, animated in the foreground and calm in the endless distance, lacking anything picturesque but of which one never grows tired, and which changes slowly under the play of the varying light. The air was mild after the hot days, the heavens were deep, and flowers perfumed the peaceful dusk. Constantin Michel gazed at the light dresses of the women, the uniforms of the officers, the crowd moving about on the terraces, and then turned his eyes towards the plain sleeping below him. In this grandiose setting the Moscow adventure was reduced to its true dimension. He was astounded that he had felt such passion there. He could no longer understand why Ariane's past had been able to move him so greatly. "Thank God," he thought, "that she didn't mislead me. Her unheard-of honesty perhaps saved me. Had she had the cunning of her Western sisters; had she played for me the charming sentimental comedy which we lend ourselves to so complacently; had she tried to make me believe that she loved me and that I, despite the undeniable experiences of her past, was the first man to enter her heart—who knows if I wouldn't have been taken in? But with her it isn't possible to sustain these illusions that take us so far. I never saw anyone more matter-of-fact. She displays herself like an anatomical plate: what women hide, she shows. I wager that upon my return from Crimea I'll know the exact number of her lovers and their civil status. I'm a number on her list, and I should never forget this. I should be grateful to that charming girl for having been willing to give me so freely the gift of herself; I should thank her for having allowed me to avoid lengthy hesitations and for having renounced the usual games."

While still in this mood he wrote her a joyful letter, admitting in the clearest terms that he couldn't live without their long conversations, which had given charm to his Moscow stay, and promised a thousand varieties of bliss in the weeks to come in Crimea. He received a note from her that crossed paths with his own. She never mentioned the proposed journey and wittily described her life caught between an amorous uncle and an aunt whose jealousy was at war with her customary indolence. Her letter had the nimble and casual tone that she brought to everything.

He sent her a telegram announcing his arrival and confirmed their departure for the following day.

Ariane Nicolaevna was waiting for him on the station

platform and affectionately cuddled against him in the coach that took them to the hotel. She had taken her final exam that very day and had passed with flying colors. She raised no objection to the Crimea trip and told him of the ingenious way, with the complicity of a friend, she had fooled her father, her uncle, her aunt Varvara, and the many friends who were expecting her in the provinces. She insisted only that she had to be back home on June 10 for the most serious reasons and that no discussion on this point was possible. She thus had one week to give her friend.

The next day the Sebastopol express took them away.

They were alone, stretched out on a small beach, with red sand hot at the water's edge. To the right, the left, and behind them the nearby rocks were jagged and red. At their feet gentle waves died with the sound of fabric being torn. In the pure sky a few small clouds filled with light remained motionless, as if hooked to the azure. Just as Constantin Michel had promised, they lived like gods, naked on the shore beneath the sun that bathed their reclining bodies, breathing in the sea air, saying not a word. They'd been near Yalta for over a week, never apart for a moment. They were living in the house that a painter friend of Constantin's had lent him, a small house with white walls and a red roof, out of the way on the rocks, not far from the road that goes from Yalta to Alushta. The house had but two rooms. One, the larger, faced south and the sea through its three windows, and had whitewashed walls on which were hung oriental fabrics; lined up against the walls were sofas covered with Persian carpets. It served as a living room and dining room. The other room, smaller but still spacious, was the bedroom. At sunset it looked out on a strange landscape of cacti, succulent plants, flowers, rocks, and pines. In the back of the house was the kitchen and the room for the maid, who prepared their meals. She was a girl with Tatar blood, with black hair and beautiful bare feet that gently glided through the house without being heard.

Ariane had walked around the house that Constantin had chosen for their life together like a cat inspecting a new home and then had vanished into the kitchen, where she had a long discussion with the Tatar girl. Constantin had charged her with managing the house, not without fear that it would be done in a fanciful fashion. He was wrong. Ariane showed herself to be an accomplished housekeeper. Not only were meals served at fixed times, but they were excellent and varied. Ariane didn't disdain giving the Tatar recipes— recipes from Varvara Petrovna's renowned cook—and watched over their execution. There was a *chaud-froid de poisson au caviar* that sent Constantin into a state of ecstasy, and a *coulibiac* that was talked about long after. The girl took her new duties seriously and, when they dined, rejoiced at seeing Constantin doing honor to the menu.

Their life flowed along, monotonously but exquisitely. They woke up late in the bright room. Ariane clapped her hands, at the sound of which the barefoot Tatar, smiling and silent, arrived, bearing a tray with chocolate, tea, cream, fresh bread, butter, and jams. They breakfasted with gusto side by side, in no hurry to get out of bed. Nevertheless, at eleven o'clock they left the large, warm bed and went to the nearby small beach. There they frolicked in the broad daylight, playing like children among the rocks, entered the tepid water, and emerged only to plunge back in, before finally stretching out nude on the hot sand. Ariane would then free her long hair. They remained motionless beneath the burning sun, their eyelids closed. It was as if the sun's rays penetrated to the center of their being. Under their skin it was as if there was the crackling of millions of tiny electric sparks. Universal life seemed to be flowing through them. They were brothers with the rocks, the sand, and the flowers that surrounded them. The salty wind caressed their bodies and passed through the toes of their bare feet. It was a long, exquisite languor; they didn't say a word. They hardly felt themselves living.

Around one o'clock, when the sun fell directly on them, they returned as if drunk to the cool room and lunched greedily. They followed this with a long siesta during the hottest hours. On the first day Constantin had stretched out on the sofa. Ariane rested on the bed, and on the second day, to his great surprise, she called for him. Reading, smoking, and sleeping, they lay this way beside each other, semiclad, and at five o'clock they took tea. They finally had to get dressed. Ariane sighed, but arranged her hair and put on a dress as light as a spiderweb.

At dusk they left their domain and walked along the Yalta road. They often went as far as the city, just a few versts way, crossing the rich orchards and flower gardens lining the banks. There, once night had fallen, they supped on the terrace of a hotel overlooking the sea. Below them boats rocked in the port illuminated by large electric globes. Distant music drifted through the balmy air. People looked with envy on this couple whose happiness was like a challenge. Finally, they returned to their villa. Along the road fireflies pierced the fragrant bushes with their points of fire that flittered from branch to branch, going out only to flame up again farther along, giving their nocturnal stroll a passionate setting, where with every step, love burned in brief and intense flames. At home they found the samovar on the table and, undressing and embracing, they stayed up talking deep into the night.

Ariane's external reserve, which she hadn't shed, disappeared in the intimacy of their life together. She now used the informal form with her lover, who had remarked that in a girl of her nature the formal form lacked simplicity. In Constantin's arms she was a tender and passionate mistress, with something refined and violent in the caresses she lavished on him.

But he sensed that deep down nothing had changed. She remained ironic, witty, with a freedom of spirit that bordered on open cynicism. The mere question that it could be a matter of love between them would have led her to burst out in insolent and juvenile laughter. Love is the pure dream of an innocent maiden. Wise ones seek in the physical the sole realities, and the extreme pleasures of sensuality have no need to be complicated by a sentimental malady apt to render the most intelligent people stupid.

And so she thanked her lover for having organized in so marvelous a fashion an existence that satisfied her senses and left her heart and mind free.

She had the delicacy, during their first week at the seaside, not to bring up her previous experiences. When she spoke of love, she did so in generalities. This wealth of materialist wisdom from Ariane's mouth contrasted strangely with the radiant youth of her eighteen years, and it never ceased to astound Constantin Michel.

And this is how, with one day following another in a never-ending and passionate series, they reached June 10, the date when Ariane was supposed to head home. And yet she had once alluded to the need to be on time for a rendezvous that she hadn't explained any further. In vain did Constantin, whose curiosity was aroused and who thought he knew everything about his mistress, try to press her on this point. She responded in vague and willfully ambiguous terms; it was a commitment she'd pledged to honor and that she had to keep. From certain things she said, he understood that there were financial issues involved. When she spoke of it she grew guarded and irritable, finally imploring Constantin to avoid the subject, which was painful for her. He kept quiet about it, but felt there was something obscure involved and would have given much to penetrate the worrisome mystery. Another week passed. Ariane looked at the calendar more often, and her mood changed.

One evening, while they were dining on the terrace of a hotel in Yalta, she spoke of their imminent, and this time definitive, separation.

"You'll again race around the world and after women, and I, next fall, will again take up my studies in Moscow at the university. I'm thinking of going to Europe after the first semester, to Paris and London."

"So we'll meet there," Constantin said joyfully. "Wait till you see what a beautiful life I'll arrange for you."

"I'll never see you again," she said, without raising her voice. "What's the point? Reheated dishes aren't worth a thing. We've lived very well together and we should leave things at that. And anyway," she continued, with a charming smile for Constantin, "I was lucky enough not to grow attached to you. I ran a great risk, since you're dangerous. I was able to avoid it. Do you see me falling in love with you? Do you want me to suffer from your absence?"

"Yes," Constantin said simply. "That's what I want."

"Well, I don't. I have my youth before me, and don't think I'll sacrifice it to you. You'll forget me quickly. Does a little girl, as you say, count on a long list? Thank God everything has gone as agreed. We're not going to start nibbling at a new morsel for which neither of us is made. Admit that you don't see me as a tearful lover. Is that a role for me? We'll bid each other farewell in a few days..."

Constantin felt his irritation growing. He looked at Ariane. She was gay and spoke in a detached tone that wounded him to the quick.

They continued to tear each other apart for some time, smiling, impassive, both seeking the enemy's weak point in order to sink in their blade. The people looking at them with envy imagined they were exchanging the thousand tender words customary to lovers. Constantin concluded on these terms: "We're right next to each other but between us there is an abyss that can't be filled. I give up trying to... Let's go."

Ariane had a pained smile at the corners of her mouth. They rose and returned to their lodging on foot. The moon played on the water and bathed the sleeping orchards of Yalta. Ariane was silent and Constantin felt an unnamed bitterness deep in his heart.

They went to bed in silence. But once in bed, as they were falling asleep, Ariane cuddled against her lover, took his face in her hands, and smothered it with kisses.

"Forgive me," she whispered in his ear. "I was wicked, and I'll never do that again."

And Constantin found again the humble, childlike voice he'd heard only once, when Ariane had given herself to him.

8. SEPARATION

A TELEGRAM arrived at lunchtime two days later. Constantin opened it and handed it to Ariane. He was recalled urgently to Moscow. Without hesitating, without consulting her—Ariane observed—he telegraphed Sebastopol to reserve a coupé for Moscow two days later. Ariane had no words of regret. That evening she was as joyful and chatty as ever.

But the next morning, as they dawdled in the warmth of the bed and seemed unable to leave it, she surprised Constantin with an unexpected declaration that, based on her past experience, she couldn't have children. Her lover remarked that for their mutual pleasure she could have told him about this sooner.

"You never asked me," she calmly answered.

Constantin thought to himself that she could go to the devil, but profited from the observation during the short time left with Ariane.

And the following day they bid the seaside house farewell, as well as the barefoot Tatar girl, who filled their automobile with flowers. That evening they took the express to Moscow, and they arrived thirty-six hours later, in the morning. Constantin had gotten Ariane to agree to spend one more day and one more night with him before their separation. They stayed at the National Hotel.

Constantin feared these final hours. He had to leave for

a long trip, having been called to New York on a difficult business matter. At another time he would have greeted this telegram with joy; like a deus ex machina in an opera, it put an end to a situation from which there was no way out. However delicious your mistress might be, you nevertheless must leave her. Fate had provided the necessary rupture and come to the rescue of Constantin, who would have struggled to find the strength to break up. Ariane had given him the flower of her youth and her spirit. Could he be angry with her for an excess of honesty so rare in women? Was he going to hold it against her that she didn't love him as others had loved him? Would he be so mad as to regret not seeing her in tears at their moment of separation? And yet this epicurean looked on her, in the waning moments of their affair, with an emotion he didn't try to hide from himself and that, on the contrary, he was ready to congratulate himself for. Mixed in was worry about what would happen, like the physical fear felt by an animal who's afraid of being beaten.

They wandered around Moscow in the afternoon. To all appearances, Ariane was living a day like any other. In the evening, she was as tender and passionate with him as during the unforgettable hours in Crimea.

But the next morning, while she was still in bed and he was getting up, the feared attack suddenly developed with great magnitude. As always, it was carried out in a detached, conversational tone.

"Well then," she said abruptly. "Tomorrow I'll be back home. You who so love to command, how many days do you order me to be faithful?"

Constantin ran to her, put his hand over her mouth, and said imploringly, "I beg you, Ariane, by everything that unites us, don't spoil the final moments we're spending together.

In a few days we'll be far from each other. I don't know what life will make of us, but be quiet. I can't bear the idea that you will ever belong to anyone but me. It's absurd, but that's how it is. I beg you, please respect these necessary illusions. I know, I know...You'll live and I have no rights over you. But later...Let's not talk any more about it...Wait; time will come to our rescue. Be quiet, little girl; one must know when not to talk."

And he smothered her in kisses, held her tightly in his arms. But when he released her from his embrace and continued dressing, she said, pitilessly, "I have a lover waiting for me. I didn't hide it from you."

This time he remained like ice, seeming not to have heard.

She continued in a low, soft voice that was a hundred leagues from the meaning of her words, "He'll call as soon as I've returned. I'm two weeks late for our rendezvous. How can I refuse myself to him? What would be the pretext? Let's say I gain a few days, a week of purification. Really, you can't ask more of me. He has rights over me, prior to yours. And you know how life is among us at home, how easy everything is, how different it all is from here...Come, let's compromise. I promise you that for a week I'll live in what you call 'our cherished memories.' But don't ask anything more of me, because, really, what's the point of such posthumous fidelity?"

Constantin fled, slamming the door, cursing and swearing along the length of the stairway. At lunch in the afternoon and until evening, when they were both on the Ryazan station platform, Ariane continued to be aggressive and irritable.

"It looks like you want to make our separation easier for me," Constantin said to her. "You don't want me to miss you, do you?"

They embraced without enthusiasm, as if carrying out a chore.

Constantin remained on the platform, watching the heavy convoy depart. He felt oppressed. He needed calm.

"Yet another chapter of my life closed, and not the least bit interesting. But it was about time..."

9. A BEAUTIFUL SUMMER

WITH ARIANE'S arrival, Varvara Petrovna's house once again became lively. Dr. Michel Ivanovich was there every day and arranged things so that he often came in the afternoon and the evening. He didn't hide his pleasure at again seeing Ariane, and Varvara Petrovna felt no jealousy. Between Olga Dimitrievna and Ariane there was the same intimacy as in the past. Olga was the only person whom Ariane kept, even at a distance, as confidant. As a result, she was aware of the unfortunate affair with the famous actor of whom all the women of Russia dreamed, and the brief but sensational adventure with Constantin Michel, whom she called the Grand Prince. The trip to Crimea, though Ariane spoke of it with the detachment she always brought to accounts of her romantic life, seemed to her embroidered in gold and silk, like tales we read of the Orient. Together they frequented the summer theater and showed themselves off on the busy terraces of the Alexander Garden. They supped with their "company," as they called it, which was no less brilliant than that of the previous year. Olga Dimitrievna even seemed no longer to fear the engineer Michel Bogdanov. During Ariane's absence he had been able to win her over. He had grown close to her because she was the sole real friend of the woman he continued to call the Queen of Sheba, about whom he spoke whenever he could. Through a thousand ingenious means, and in particular through gifts, to which Olga was quite receptive, he had succeeded in attaching her to himself. He had convinced her that he had for Ariane not a passing fancy but the most serious sentiments, and that he counted on the latter to become, whenever she wanted, Mme Michel Bogdanova. In all her letters Olga boasted of the merits of the engineer, his generosity and the superiority of his intelligence, and congratulated Ariane Nicolaevna on her conquest of him. Olga no longer put up any obstacles to the rendezvous that the engineer requested with Ariane.

What is strange is that the latter continued to see him at his home twice a week, but at twilight, in order to avoid any repeat of the scandal of the previous year. She often arrived at the small suburban house accompanied by Olga Dimitrievna, whom she left at the door.

As soon as she entered, Ariane unhooked her wristwatch, a gift from Constantin Michel, and placed it on a commode right in the middle of everything.

"It's exactly six o'clock," she said.

After an hour, never more, she would be seen leaving the house, Olga Dimitrievna joking with her about her strict accounting, never adding a minute to the sixty she owed the engineer.

"Business is business, and what better place to be precise if it's not in relations with your banker?" Ariane said with no hesitation.

Varvara Petrovna observed her niece. She found her changed, more serious.

"There's something new about you—" she said, "new and undefinable. You're not in love, are you?"

The supposition was so insane that Ariane burst into

laughter. "It's a sickness that doesn't afflict those of my age, but of yours," she teasingly replied to her aunt.

Nicolas Ivanov had been gone from the city for three months. He hadn't been seen all winter, having shut himself in on his property. He had then left for Crimea, where supposedly his mother's health required his presence. But it was said that his mind was unhinged and that he was himself under treatment with the specialist who took care of Mme Ivanovna *mère*. Postcards addressed to Ariane arrived every day; she tossed them out without reading them.

She was being courted by a handsome young man, whom she played a thousand tricks on and whom she cruelly mocked.

Varvara Petrovna wasn't wrong in remarking that her niece had changed. It appeared she was leading the life she had the previous year, but she no longer brought the same carefree enthusiasm to it that had made her famous throughout town. To be sure, she was still the most sparkling supper companion in the Alexander Garden. She had never spared anyone, but her raillery now seemed crueler; the knife thrusts now struck deeper. Neither people nor theories could withstand her rash criticisms. Like Mephistopheles in Goethe's *Faust*, she could have said, "I am the spirit that negates all." Even so, she went out less frequently. She remained at home, daydreaming on her sofa. She thought of Constantin Michel. He was different from the men who surrounded her, even in his attire, even in a certain ease of manner that allowed him to do virtually anything without descending into vulgarity. But it was to other qualities that he owed the place he occupied in her thoughts, the front-rank position she granted him. She sensed in him a constant force she didn't control. She played with other men for an instant and then, disgusted before growing tired of them, she let them return to the void. Things were different with Constantin. She hadn't amused herself with him, but he with her. It's certain that at moments she'd exasperated him, but he hadn't lost his detestable sangfroid for a single minute. And what had she gained in all this? Had he attached himself more profoundly than one normally does to a beautiful young girl to whom gives one pleasure? He had taken her when he wanted her and left her on the day he chose. She had given herself at the time he had appointed and she hadn't missed a single one of their rendezvous at the National Hotel. But he had once, at the last minute, been daring enough to cancel on her, and she had come back the following day. He had left for Kiev at his own convenience and had taken her to Crimea when it pleased him. She had stayed there two weeks beyond the brief time at her disposal, but Constantin, the minute the telegram calling him back had arrived, had determined their departure date without consulting her. He had abandoned her in Moscow without granting her a day of grace, which, in any case, she wouldn't have asked for had it cost her her life. Olga Dimitrievna was right: she had been weak enough to allow him to see that she recognized his superior rights. He ordered; she obeyed.

This phrase in Ariane's mouth caused her to go pale with rage. "What must he think of me? He treats me like his slave. Where is he now? Which women is he winning by his infernal assurance? If I ever see him again he'll pay dearly for the humiliations he dared make me suffer. I'll take my vengeance."

This was Ariane's state of mind when one day she received a laconic telegram. It was datelined New York and read:

WILL BE IN MOSCOW IN A MONTH. SEE YOU SOON. CONSTANTIN MICHEL, PLAZA HOTEL.

"He's not even polite enough to add 'tenderly,' or 'a thousand kisses,'" she growled furiously. "Of course I won't see him. Who does he take me for? Does he think I'm waiting for him? God save me from answering this insolent telegram."

The telegram had arrived around noon. In the evening, she went out accompanied by one of her male friends. She had never been so amiable with this insignificant young man, who, to hear Ariane tell, and seeing the way she looked at him, had no doubt that he'd finally attained the happiness he'd so long hoped for. They strolled in the evening in the Dvoranskaya.

As they returned home and passed before the telegraph office, Ariane suddenly said, "Excuse me a minute."

She pushed open the door and went into the office. He followed her. She quickly wrote down Constantin Michel's address in New York and, beneath the address, just one word:

HURRAH

Without signing it, she tossed the telegram onto the counter along with some money, and fled as if pursued.

10. RESUMPTION

ARIANE was back in Moscow in the first days of September. She'd given up on living with her uncle and aunt and was living with a good woman who rented her a well-furnished room in a modern apartment where she could receive her friends and organize those gatherings of young people that students of both sexes are so fond of in Russia. They gave themselves over to the delights of passionate ideological discussions that went on far into the night, where as many ideas are exchanged as cups of tea are drunk. Subtlety and the absolute mingle at these events in the most paradoxical fashion, and in their discussions, dogmatism is as present as life experience is absent. And all the while the students court the young girls, as always happens with young people in every country and at every latitude.

Ariane hadn't had any further news of Constantin Michel. When she had obtained her lodgings, she left her address and phone number for him at his hotel. But weeks had passed, and on a day when she was feeling resentful towards him, she had tried to retrieve the note. The doorman had refused to hand over to this unknown woman the correspondence of a well-known client. "What I'll have to do if he comes here is send word that I'm away," she said to herself.

On this late afternoon she was alone at her house when the phone rang. She had a foreboding that the "Grand Prince," as Olga Dimitrievna called him, was at the other end of the line. She blanched and decided not to answer. But on their own her legs carried her to the telephone. She picked up the receiver and said in a clear voice, "Hello."

And without asking who was on the line, a male voice at the other end cried joyously, "I'm finally here, and I'm waiting for you without a minute of delay. Take the fastest horse and give a royal tip."

She hung up, ran to her mirror, straightened out her hair, and was about to leave the apartment when she changed her mind. She went back into her room, hurried to her bureau, opened a drawer, and in the disorder of the papers looked for a dirty sheet, folded it, slipped it into her reticule, and left.

Fifteen minutes later she knocked on Constantin's door. On the way she had prepared a nasty phrase, but when she saw the Grand Prince standing before her with open arms, her tongue betrayed her and she was surprised to hear herself say, "Well, monsieur, you certainly have kept me waiting."

The dined sitting side by side at Constantin's place, and he barely had time to bring her up to date on his affairs. Ariane didn't listen to him, as she was filled with joy in recounting and describing the splendid life she'd lived during the summer in her southern kingdom. She made the successive splendors pass before the Grand Prince's eyes. When they finished eating she was surprised to find Constantin preparing to go out and asking her to get dressed.

"We're going to your house," he said.

"You can't come to my place, and you're never going to go there. What do you want to go there for?"

"Silly girl," said Constantin. "Don't you know that I'm keeping you here tonight? But at the hotel, with the blessed police regulations, you have to leave your passport at the desk. Let's go get it."

Ariane was embarrassed. "As it happens, I have it with me."

She opened her reticule and pulled out the sheet she'd taken from the drawer.

They fell asleep in the same bed. Three months of separation had torn them from each other and cast them into civilizations so opposed that they seemed to inhabit different planets. Where had they come from at this moment when they finally found each other again? Thanks to Ariane's vivid tales, Constantin saw as if with his own eyes the southern capital of which she was the sovereign. He even knew the physical and moral particularities of her entourage. But she remained impenetrable. What mysterious forces had driven her here and there? Whom had she found in that city he detested? With what attitude had she approached her old friends? What new acquaintances had she made? He knew nothing. And for her part, Ariane couldn't imagine the atmosphere in which the Grand Prince had lived. He had always been sparing in details about himself. Even so, she was not unaware of the way he looked at women. Was there any need to learn more?

There they were, lying alongside each other, tired, on the edge of sleep. But they were thinking so intensely that it seemed to both of them that their thoughts were being externalized and would become visible to their nearby immobile adversary. "Can it be that she doesn't know what's going on within me?" Constantin thought. And trembling, Ariane thought, "Please God, let me not betray myself and allow him to read my heart."

They finally fell asleep.

11. LIFE AS A COUPLE

THEIR life organized itself on its own without their having worked out a plan. Ariane went to the university during the day, and Constantin to his business. He had taken an office in the center of the city. They lived together, but Ariane kept her room, and in doing so she kept up appearances, had an address in Moscow, and received friends at her home. At the hotel, Constantin had chosen a larger, three-room apartment. Nevertheless, they continued to share a bedroom, and Ariane, on her own authority, had had one of the beds removed. The one that remained wasn't large, but "I'm thin," she said, "and I won't bother you." The sitting room served as an office for Constantin, and the second bedroom was set up as a dining room.

They went their own ways in the morning and met again at dinner, which they more often than not took at home. But Ariane sometimes asked to go to one of Moscow's elegant restaurants. There she refused to eat in a private room, as Constantin would have preferred, for he feared displaying her and in doing so, compromising her. She had family and friends in Moscow. She belonged to the wealthy and enlightened bourgeoisie; she was barely eighteen. Shouldn't she make a few sacrifices in order to maintain her social position? But Ariane, with a haughty lack of concern, showed disdain for any rumors that might arise from her adventure. Never had anyone been more indifferent to the opinion of others. She took pleasure wherever she found it and let the people talk. She was concerned with saving face only with the small number of students with whom she was friends; with them she took precautions. Thanks to the complicity of her landlady, for a long time no one in her circle suspected the double life she lived, for these young, impecunious people didn't frequent fashionable restaurants. When Ariane received phone calls the landlady invariably answered that she had just left. Friday evenings her friends came to her place. Constantin, who didn't have much patience, had decided that these weekly gatherings would end early enough for Ariane to make it to the hotel by one o'clock in the morning. He had imposed this condition with the unwavering quality he brought to everything, and against which Ariane, whatever her independence of character, never rebelled. But in Russia, how is one to send one's friends away when they are gathered at one's home? Ariane laid out the difficulties before the Grand Prince. He answered that it was up to her to figure it out; that if they came home at one o'clock they wouldn't be asleep before two or half past two, and that he wasn't about to change his habits for a few night owl students. Since she insisted so strongly, he added ill-humoredly that his door would be closed at the indicated hour and that if she stayed out beyond it she could always sleep at her own home. Ariane listened to him in silence and reflected. She was surprised by Constantin's attitude towards her. She found hateful the way he affected to treat her like a free person, leaving her a choice on every occasion, even as he exercised limitless tyranny over her. She tried to console herself with the thought that Constantin was more attached to her than he cared to show. If he was not, why would he insist on her returning at a set time? But why, in the same breath, did he offer to remain at her home until the morning? She rebelled in words but submitted in deeds, hating herself for her cowardice. Every week she promised herself that she would prolong her reception, forget the hour, and finally sleep, at least once, in her student flat. But every Friday, well before midnight, she showed signs of nervousness, constantly looking at her watch, a present from the Grand Prince. Supper was served at nine o'clock, she allowed the conversation to drag on, put a stop to the games, and before midnight found a thousand pretexts to dismiss her guests.

She arrived, her cheeks pink from the cold, her eyes glowing beneath her fur hat, gangly, childlike, full of amusing anecdotes and witty expressions. When she entered the room where Constantin was lying on a sofa, daydreaming or reading or smoking a cigarette, youth entered with her. They had tea and talked. She told of the evening she'd just passed. To hear her tell, what *didn't* happen at those Friday gatherings? On those days Ariane's room became the center of the most passionate adventures. All of Moscow life seemed to be concentrated there. As she undressed she painted the actors in just a few words, tracing unforgettable figures. And then, in bed, she finished telling her amazing stories. Constantin listened to her, filled with wonder. He sometimes thought, "Wouldn't it be wise to remain in this room and send this little girl around the world, from which she'd bring you every evening the most colorful and varied portraits? The most ordinary object, when looked at through this child's eyes, radiates beauty."

As time passed Ariane attended her university courses with less regularity. In the morning she lingered in bed. She now got up at noon, dragged out her ablutions, and was rarely ready before half past one. Then she had to have lunch. The day was almost over when they rose from the table. She then asked to accompany Constantin on his errands, leading him to the doorway where he was expected. She refused to take a sled and leapt around the Grand Prince like a puppy around its master. Sometimes she went ahead of him, strolling a few steps in advance, acting mischievously, stopping before shopwindows, making faces at passersby, turning around to look when a handsome officer passed, chatting with a schoolchild, and then running to catch up with Constantin. Holding on to his arm, and raising her face to his, she would burst out laughing, mocking the men and women who passed.

"You resemble the Olympian Jupiter," she said to him, "a Jupiter exiled in Scythia and forced to wear furs. I would give anything to see the master of the gods slip on the ice and buy a theater ticket in the stalls. I beg you, do me a favor and just once lie down flat in the middle of the Marshals' Bridge."

Constantin felt like he was being dragged along by a violent current. At first he'd tried to make Ariane see reason, to get her to continue her courses. At times, he reproached himself for destroying the young girl's career. At other times, when he was wiser, he reproached himself for his fears. How could anyone want to imprison so rich a nature in such a narrow frame? One day she would suddenly leave him, for no reason, just as she had taken him. She'd do extravagant things, or things the world considers reasonable. But whatever happened, she'd be an unending source of life.

12. *SEMPER EADEM*

In their new life as a couple, while the ties of the flesh and the spirit that united them became, without their feeling them grow, more numerous and stronger by the day, their sentimental positions remained as they had been at the beginning of their relationship, and the latent drama between them developed, taking on a tragic intensity.

Both strove mightily to prove to themselves that they weren't in love, that between them was nothing but an adventure in which pleasure was the beginning and the end.

Ariane executed variations of a peerless virtuosity on this theme. One day she started dancing with joy in the middle of the room.

"What's the matter with you?" Constantin said.

"I'm happy," she answered. "I feel free and gay. You know, I could have suffered a catastrophe; I could have loved you. I would have become sentimental." She raised her eyes to the heavens and joined her hands. "I would have sighed." She sighed deeply. "I would have lost my joyfulness. I would have become as silly as my aunt is with her handsome doctor. I wouldn't be able to part from you; I would wait for you, moaning. I'd be so foolish as to smother you with declarations that would cause you to be disgusted. I'd be tortured with jealousy. I'd spy on you, surprising you in your office. I'd want to know where you went, which women you met in society. I'd call you in the houses you frequent. I'd end up making myself ridiculous... Perhaps I'd even cry." She wiped her eyes. "Do you see me with my eyes red with tears? Thank God I won't know these horrors. I thank you, Grand Prince, for not having sought to take hold of my heart. I don't know how to express my gratitude for having raised pleasure so high that on its own it is enough, and for having succeeded in preserving it in its purest state. You are a true artist. I bow before you. You are the master."

And she kneeled before him, lowering her forehead to the rug at his feet, rising, performing a thousand ceremonial genuflections.

Other times she said, "I have to confess something to you. Once or twice I thought I was defeated. How frightened I was. How I would have suffered at the moment we separated from each other. What a battle I fought against myself. But I regained control of myself. Since I've resisted you for so long, the game is won. Hurrah!"

While she expounded these unvarying themes, Constantin listened to her closely, weighing every word, attentive to the least nuance, to the sound of her voice, to the tone of her sentences, to the accent of her words. Was she sincere? Was she trying to mislead him? He never discovered a false note. She seemed to express herself with total sincerity.

He limited himself to responding, "Little girl, whether you like it or not, you love me. You are entering the eternally prescribed cycle of your sex: you are the slave."

Depending on the day, Ariane broke out in laughter, or shrugged her left shoulder, or became angry.

Sometimes she said to him, "And you, do you love me?"

The first time she asked him that question, Constantin was surprised. But he didn't show his astonishment. He rose from the chair in which he was seated, approached the girl standing before him, took her in his arms, and in a caressingly reproachful voice said to her, "My child, don't even think of it. How could you imagine that I love a wicked little girl like you?"

Ariane was left speechless. What should she believe? The ironic words or the caressing tone? Constantin forever eluded her. The moment she thought she had him in her grasp, with a sudden leap he slipped from between her fingers. What were the men she'd known before compared with him? In a short time she had turned the proudest of them into slaves who submitted to her least caprice. Constantin was an adversary worthy of her, and confusing. Why did he affect with her the tender, jocular tone used with children?

She tried to make him jealous. She painted an enchanting portrait of one of the students who attended her Friday soirees. No woman could resist him. And he was madly in love with her...

"That boy's got good taste" was all Constantin said.

"He tried to kiss me the other evening..."

"It's his duty as a man."

"So it probably wouldn't make any difference to you, would it?"

"Dear little girl," Constantin then said. "Nothing would be easier than for you to cheat on me. But what would be the point? If you don't love me, what are you doing here? Why remain with me? But if you love me—and that's obvious—what pleasure would you find in the arms of another? I haven't lived with you for eight months without having gotten to know you. You had and you will have other affections, but you're loyal. There is something proud and rare in your character. You'll leave me one day, but you'll never cheat on me."

Ariane listened attentively to her lover's speech, seeking to make out what was hidden beneath his words. His tone was never passionate. He didn't seem to mix any sentiment into his conversations about romantic casuistry. Was it a matter of him or of her? It was hard to be sure.

She maintained her hold on Constantin Michael on one point alone. She'd discovered it on the fifth day of their relationship and since then had made marvelous use of her discovery. The Grand Prince wanted Ariane's past to remain shrouded. According to the unwritten laws that govern the empire of love, these are things that are never spoken of. There are necessary illusions that every woman knows how to maintain. Ariane insisted on casting a crude light on her past.

But the severity with which Constantin stopped her whenever she broached this forbidden subject now forced her to resort to cunning in order to reach the desired result. Her clever mind provided her a thousand roundabout ways by which she managed to torment the Grand Prince. She had told him of her recent relationship with the famous actor from the Art Theater. Without risking disclosing any dangerous specifics, she was certain he no longer had any doubt concerning her relations with him. At regular but frequent intervals, she arranged things so the actor appeared before Constantin in their conversations. They would be talking about the dramatic arts and suddenly the name of that former lover came up out of nowhere in the conversation. She explained his merits, characterized his talent, analyzed his preferred roles, described his costumes, his makeup, the way he came onstage, the magnificent bearing he gave certain classical characters. It goes without saying that she spoke of all this only as the spectator of an actor. She would eventually see a familiar wrinkle form on Constantin's brow, and the latter would end by saying dryly, "Actors don't interest me. There's no emptier subject of conversation."

Ariane would then gloat inside, but she avoided allowing it to be seen that she had carried off a victory.

For a long time she insisted that they go together to applaud this hero in this or that play in his repertoire. Constantin absolutely refused. Ariane went back on the attack. Finally Constantin said to her one day, "If you want to go to the Art Theater, I'll get a seat for you. If you want someone to accompany you, invite one of your lover boys and I'll get two. That evening I'll dine at Mme X——'s home; she's been asking me to do so for some time."

Because she spoke so often about the actor, she succeeded in bringing him to life in Constantin's mind. The actor was Ariane's "last lover." She had left his arms to fall into his own. It was to the actor that she had told the extraordinary story of her life. He had been able to hold on to this scornful girl for three months. What kind of man was he? What airs did he put on with women? Constantin felt that he wouldn't completely know Ariane until he'd seen with his own eyes the predecessor who, whether he willed it or not, haunted his thoughts. But it would be impossible for him to go to the theater one evening with Ariane and be seated in front of a stage where suddenly, with all the prestige of a grand actor, he would appear before them to the applause of spectators. The girl, in her infernal ploys, had shaken his nerves to the point that he felt incapable of bearing up under such a trial. And yet he had to see this man. It was only in this way that he would free himself from the nightmare in which he was living. He kept an eye on the theater posters. One Friday he read the well-known name on the program and reserved a seat, certain of having the evening free, since Ariane was receiving her friends in her student room.

He dined early and alone, irritated with Ariane and himself, and then headed off on foot for the theater. He walked quickly, absorbed in his thoughts, not feeling the thirty-below-zero temperature that stung his face. Reaching the vestibule he opened his fur-lined cloak and took out his ticket. He gave a sudden start. He tore up the ticket, threw the pieces to the ground, and, going out onto the street, hailed a sleigh. He noted with surprise that he was perspiring. He was breathing heavily. "I avoided quite an act of cowardice," he said aloud.

13. THE FEMALE FRIEND

HE BLURTED an address to the coachman and the sleigh sped over the hardened snow.

He went to the home of a young woman whom he had met at the home of Baroness Korting. The latter was spending the winter in Pau for her health. Natasha X——, whom he was going to see, was the young wife of an officer posted in Mongolia. She lived isolated in a small house in the Arbat quarter in the company of an old aunt of her husband. She was a charming creature, at times gay, at times melancholic, who at seventeen had made a foolish marriage to a fast-living and penurious officer she didn't love. She could have left him or taken a lover, but Natasha had never had the courage. She had married upon leaving the Imperial Institute, knowing nothing of life. In the arms of a brutal and impatient husband she had conceived the most unfortunate idea of love. She hadn't forgotten the tears shed on the express train taking her to the Caucasus. Nothing had erased that first impression. Since then her husband had grown tired of her. He had himself sent on distant missions, and at twenty Natasha lived a sad life, quasi-abandoned, hesitant, worried, and yet with a hint of a smile at the corners of her young lips. At first sight, what they called a tender friendship was born between her and Constantin. In Russia, a country where people live freely, liberated from all conventions, indifferent to what people may say, where education, reduced to an apprenticeship in good manners, honors natural spontaneity, no one is surprised to see feelings blossom quickly and manifest with such simplicity. The first time they met, Natasha had spoken to Constantin as she'd never spoken to anyone before. The second time they spoke, she'd joked with him about his relationship with a student, "a ravishing one, I've heard." Constantin was greatly surprised to learn that the details of his private life, which he'd mentioned to no one, were known in the salon of Baroness Korting. He denied nothing, judging it wise to appear not to grant any importance to baseless rumors. Natasha gradually returned to the subject, which seemed to interest her, and Constantin responded with a few brief, enigmatic phrases. And yet several times he had let his irritation show at both the girl's difficult character, and the duel with hidden weapons they'd engaged in from the start. But he always did so in veiled terms, never revealing himself. Natasha listened to him attentively. Her sly questions were all aimed at the same goal: she wanted to know Constantin's feeling for Ariane. Constantin avoided the question. Natasha burned to meet the young girl. When she spoke of this for the first time to Constantin Michel, he shrugged. She didn't allow herself to be discouraged and returned to the attack, assaulting him every time they met. She succeeded so well that Constantin was forced to promise to discuss the matter with Ariane. He kept his promise and, with some hemming and hawing, approached the subject one day when he had a box at the ballet.

He was met with a categorical refusal from Ariane, who knew Natasha by sight and who found her, it should be said, lovely and pleasant.

She answered Constantin Michel with the sharpness with

which she always responded to him. "I have no desire to satisfy the curiosity of your girlfriends. Why do they want to see me? Because I'm your mistress? Thank you very much, but I don't put myself on display. And anyway, in general I hope that you never speak of me ..."

Nevertheless, Constantin spoke of her to Natasha. The sharper the conflict between him and Ariane grew, the more he felt the need to discuss the question that never ceased tormenting him. He didn't allude to his mistress, but he discoursed with Natasha on the young Russian girl of the last generation. He said to her one day: "Do you know about the free-love leagues that have been formed in the upper classes of girls' gymnasiums, particularly in the south and the Caucasus? On one of my trips, by chance, I met some young girls who revealed to me the raison d'être, the—how shall I say?—program of these leagues. It's strange. These girls, most of them quite intelligent, think that Russia must give the world a new civilization, and that it should be the first to shed the prejudices that have oppressed society for thirty centuries. These nihilistic little girls declare that the most absurd and tyrannical of prejudices is that of virginity. They don't say, 'By virtue of what rule must a girl arrive intact at her wedding?' for it would insult them to discuss marriage, which they have long since formed a negative opinion of. They say, 'Women, like men, have the right to dispose of their bodies. They will make it a subject of experiments, if that's what they want. They'll use it for their pleasure and at their convenience. There is no morality of love.' You see how these young minds construct beautiful theories, and I don't concern myself with them at all. But I'd like to know at what precise point the conflict breaks out between theory and practice. I've been assured that the most intelligent of these girls, impelled by a fanatical logic, made it a point of honor to give themselves without love and even without pleasure in order to prove to themselves their total independence. Only then were they certain of having vanquished ancient prejudices, not in words, but in deeds. This country is truly the most passionate field of experiments imaginable."

"Yes, but if one of these very wise, very mad girls comes upon a real man, she becomes a slave," Natasha responded. "Didn't you recently experience this? You know more about this than I. I was a white goose when I married, and that clearly didn't do me any good. If I had a daughter how would I raise her? I think I'd toss a coin and play heads or tails. I look at all this with far less severity than you. Life is so difficult that I'm not disposed to condemn in advance those who seek a solution to so many ills."

It must be noted that Constantin Michel and Natasha saw each other only at the home of a mutual friend. Until this point, despite the friendship he felt for the young woman, he had never paid her a visit, fearing the ease with which their relations could, from one moment to the next, change character. He sensed that Natasha was attracted to him, and it was nice to think, at the moment when the battle he was waging with Ariane was becoming more violent and painful, that if he was led to break it off with his mistress, he'd find a safe shelter in the Arbat in which to take refuge.

At those times when he was most irritated with Ariane, in the moments of anger that she loved to provoke through the cold cynicism with which she spoke of herself, Constantin often wondered how he could bear living with a little girl who was already spoiled and who, despite the charms of her youth and the prestige of her sparkling wit, was wicked to the depths of her soul. Was it man's strange weakness before the unknown? Was it fear of tomorrow, or horror before the void that overcame him? Was he at that moment in life when one hesitates to reject what one possesses out of fear of not finding better? Constantin had wondered about this often, but every time his growing intimacy with Natasha had produced a favorable response. If he so desired, tomorrow he would have a new and charming mistress. And the certainty he had when he was with Natasha that he was still pleasing gave him more assurance and calmness in the duel with Ariane.

"But then," he wondered, "if, despite her insolence, despite her wickedness, despite my occasional disgust with her, I keep her at my side, it must be that there is between us a secret and very powerful bond. What philter has that young witch had me drink?"

Nevertheless, he didn't want to make a commitment to Natasha, and saw her rarely.

So, in the sleigh that took him from the Art Theater, he was surprised to note that without thinking he had given the driver his tender friend's address.

The ground-floor windows of Natasha's home were illuminated. The domestic led him into a vast, poorly furnished sitting room. A few minutes later, Natasha entered.

She was wearing a large white robe and had thrown a light, brightly colored shawl over her shoulders. Her hair hung loose, framing a pure face. Her brown laughing eyes shone with pleasure. She offered her hands to Constantin, approached close enough to touch him, and said, in a musical voice whose gentleness he knew well, "What a surprise to see you here. To what drama do I owe your presence? But you could have telephoned me. I would have prepared a reception worthy of you and would have done my hair in your honor. Let's get out of here; it's cold and somber. Come to my room."

She led him by the hand to a small room, an entire side of which was taken up by a sofa. A samovar was soon brought in and began to whisper in the silence. A table was covered with preserves, honey, candies, and fruits. Natasha sat next to her friend. At times, when she leaned over, he saw under her gaping robe the firm contours of her breasts. A light scent reached him. He felt happy, relaxed, far from daily battles, in an atmosphere of tenderness from which a hint of sensuality was not absent. He took the young woman's hand and, from time to time, put it to his lips. They spoke without rhyme or reason, lightly, of everything under the sun. Natasha, who was observing him, asked no indiscreet questions. Time flowed without their measuring its rhythm. As it grew late, Constantin pulled his friend to him and put his arm around her. He kissed her neck. She scarcely resisted.

"What are you doing?" she asked, adding in a weak voice, "I'm afraid."

14. THE SMALL HOUSE IN THE SUBURBS

IT WAS late when he returned to the hotel. His heart was heavy, as at the approach of a tragedy. "She's already returned," he thought. "What will she have thought when she didn't find me at home?" He opened the sitting room door. He was in the darkness; only a ray of light coming from the next room filtered through the door, slightly ajar. He went into the brightly lit dining room and then into the bedroom. Ariane wasn't there. And yet he saw on the bed, thrown carelessly, her hat and her fur coat. "What happened?" he wondered. He was gripped by a mortal terror. For no reason, he feared the worst. He ran to the bathroom; it was empty.

He called out, "Ariane, Ariane!"

No one answered. He returned to the sitting room and turned on the light. Ariane was lying on the sofa, her face buried in a cushion, her hair spread out. She had snuggled up in a plaid shawl and, huddled against herself, looked like a little girl of twelve, abandoned by all, overcome with despair.

He kneeled near her, wanted to kiss her. She resisted. He tried to make her turn over.

"Leave me alone!" she said. "Get away from me!"

Constantin picked her up and tried to look at her. But she buried her face in his neck, and as he carried her to her room, he felt hot drops glide down his neck. She was crying.

He lay her on the bed and began to cover her with kisses. But she suddenly straightened up, laughed, then shouted, "Not bad acting, eh? What do you think?"

He was stunned, while in a mocking voice she explained that she could cry real tears at will, and that if an imbecilic family hadn't prevented her from going onstage, she would have had a fabulous career as an actress.

"Why was I too weak to listen to X——?" she whimpered. "He wanted to take me with him, take me on as his student. I would have made my debut at the Art Theater. I'd be famous today…"

An hour later, angry, she fell asleep at the edge of the mattress. But in the morning, she awoke in her lover's arms.

For some time Constantin had noted that the young girl often had moments of sadness. She sometimes went an entire evening without saying a word, without reading, curled up on the sofa, wrapped in a large shawl. If he questioned her, she responded, "It's nothing. Don't pay any attention."

Other times she said, "I've got some problems; don't worry about me."

If he pushed her, she refused to clarify matters, leaving it to be understood that she'd received a disagreeable letter, that difficult-to-resolve material questions had arisen that were no concern of his. Piecing together the snatches of facts wrested from her confused responses, and recalling a scene they'd had in Crimea, Constantin tried to guess the secret Ariane wanted to hide from him. He suspected an enigmatic and dark tale in which money played a role.

And then suddenly one evening he learned the truth.

During the day Ariane had refused to go out, remaining

silent and hostile, speaking a few words that were so disagreeable that Constantin, irritated, had left her alone at the hotel and dined at a restaurant with a friend. He returned early. She hadn't opened her mouth all evening, reading poetry by Pushkin as she lay on the sofa.

They'd gone to bed. And now, the lamp off, close to each other on the narrow bed, they sought sleep. Suddenly Constantin thought he heard a muffled sigh. He didn't move. Ariane trembled with tiny, nervous movements that she tried in vain to suppress. Once again, an unbearable anguish gripped his heart. He again tried to fall asleep. More than anything he feared these scenes in the night. When he couldn't see Ariane's insolent eyes and her mocking lips, when he felt near him the youth of that childlike body, he grew weak and felt he was ready to commit every possible act of cowardice. But that evening it was impossible for him to sleep. The impending drama was unavoidable. He took the girl in his arms and said to her, "What's the matter?"

"I feel sad," she said, hugging herself to him.

He pressed her, but she refused to answer.

"No, I can't. If I tell you the truth, you won't love me. You'll throw me out . . . It's something terrible."

These words upset Constantin. "Ah," he thought. "She probably cheated on me. In a moment of rage, after one of our many arguments, she threw herself into the arms of another man, and today she can't live with that burden. May I have the strength to listen to her and may God give me the courage to break with her and put an end to these tortures. Let her finally speak and I'll uproot her from me."

Torn by conflicting emotions, trembling at the idea of losing Ariane, he would have preferred to put off the decisive explanation. At the same time, he burned to know the truth.

He tried to reassure his mistress, to persuade her that he would be full of indulgence and that only lies would make their separation unavoidable. He finally led her to confess. But, broken down in sobs, she couldn't tell the tale. He had to guess, to ask questions.

The subject was money.

"What do you think I live on?" she asked.

"I don't know. You never let me broach the subject. Probably what your wealthy aunt gives you."

"My aunt never gave me a sou."

There was a long silence.

"Just a little more," Constantin thought, tense with sorrow, "and I'll know everything."

Finally, in tiny phrases wrung from her with difficulty, she told of her disputes with her father and aunt that past summer, and her appeal to the engineer.

"I thought—do you believe me?—that without giving anything of myself, I could purchase my independence by lending my body. The goal I wanted to reach justified everything in my eyes ... I wasn't selling myself. If I'd wanted to I could have made a fortune. But no, I determined on my own the sum needed to live at the university: two hundred rubles a month. Had I accepted one sou more I would have felt contempt for myself, but this way I thought I'd remain free."

Little by little the details came, precise, clear. The number of rendezvous, the strictly limited time she passed in the little house in the suburbs, her obligation to return home from vacation on a set date. She hadn't understood the horror of her position until she met Constantin: she would have wanted to be his alone. But the other man was waiting for her. She had to pay and honor her commitment.

After two hours of dialogue in the night, in tears she

begged Constantin not to allow her to leave for the south or to throw her out right away, as she deserved.

Constantin was horrified, suffocating with disgust. A phrase constantly rose to his lips, but died there: "What filth, what filth." She had constructed an unpassable barrier between them. At the moment when he'd take her in his arms, how could he forget that she had surrendered to the caresses of an invalid? It was all over between them. And yet his soul was overflowing with pity. Ariane's error was one of judgment. She hadn't sinned in her heart. She was closer to him than she'd ever been—this at the moment he was going to leave her.

Prey to an emotion he couldn't control, he held her to him, caressing her, seeking to ease her pain. He wanted to talk to her, but the only words he could find were "My poor little one...My dear heart." And for the first time the two lovers cried in each other's arms, until, crushed by fatigue, at dawn sleep finally took hold of them.

15. FARTHER ALONG

THE NIGHT following his mistress's confession, once the lamp had been extinguished, Constantin returned to the previous night's conversation. Feigning indifference, he said to her, "When you made that arrangement last year, you were no longer a virgin?"

Her initial reaction was one of revolt. Then, calming down, "No," she softly said.

"You had a lover at the time?"

"Yes."

"And that lover was the first?"

She said wickedly, "Leave me alone. It's none of your business."

But Constantin, his heart wounded, continued coldly, "You know full well that you now have nothing to hide from me. And I am made in such a way that I can't live without knowing the truth. Tell me this, then. Your lover at the time wasn't your first?"

"No," Ariane said. "No."

Constantin didn't flinch. But every word Ariane said entered him as if he were being stabbed. He did a count in his head. "Four lovers, then. The first, unknown; the second, who possessed her at the moment of the drama; the third, a banker; the fourth, the actor at the Art Theater. Plus those I'm not aware of and that I'll know before I leave her. She's eighteen. She hasn't wasted any time. And she's also known how to earn a living. She's a ravishing girl, but she's a girl . . ."

Nevertheless, in the night that enveloped them, his arm around Ariane's supple torso, he continued to converse with her in a flat, detached voice. He worked at torturing himself. It was as if he wanted to see just how much suffering he could put up with. Or rather, he compared himself to a surgeon who, possessed by the desire to study a difficult case, scalpel in hand, performs a dangerous operation on himself.

"I don't really understand," he said. "And yet there are obscure, interesting things. Explain them to me, please. When you were in the little house in the suburbs did you break up with your lover of the time? Or did you think that you had the right to return to his home that very day?"

"How can you ask me such a thing?" Ariane asked indignantly. "I was sick when I left the house in the suburbs. I went back to my aunt. I was trembling with fever. Olga Dimitrievna put me in bed. She kissed me endlessly. Pasha brought me tea. She cried without knowing why. I beg you, don't interrogate me anymore. I have to forget what happened."

Christmas came without Ariane leaving Moscow. Two days later Constantin saw a telegram lying open on the girl's handbag. He took it without thinking. It contained only these words:

WHEN ARE YOU COMING? YOU'VE MISSED THE AGREED-UPON DATE.

Ariane wasn't there. He crumpled the telegram into a ball and tossed it into the wastebasket.

Christmas! Yes, it was in her contract that she'd spend the vacation with the man she called her "banker." She was failing to meet her obligations. He ground his teeth at the thought that she could leave him to go to the little house in the suburbs.

He saw her arrive at dusk, the door opening straightaway. She came in, taking from her arm the bracelet he'd put there. "It's six o'clock," she said. She hadn't hidden from him any details of these rendezvous. He was suffocating with rage and disgust. And yet, since he was going to break up with her, why had he kept her in Moscow? Was he obeying a feeling of pity in the face of the girl's distress? What strange weakness impelled him to prolong their relationship by a few days? Hadn't he suffered enough? He recalled the irresistible impulse that had led him one evening to Baroness Korting. Why hadn't he remained with that charming woman? He had returned to Ariane and they'd gone to Crimea together. Even in New York, so far from her, he had trembled with joy at the thought that his affairs would lead him back to Moscow. And then an entire winter of cruel struggles, of merciless hand-to-hand combat . . .

And now his cup was filled to the brim. He had decided. He had been able to hold on to her a few days longer, but he felt that since learning of the little house in the suburbs, he could no longer live with her. He was already devising a trip to Petersburg. He'd leave alone and not return. Just a little more patience, the time needed to arrange his affairs. Perhaps a few weeks? What difference did it make; he could wait. In any case, what did he now have to fear?

Ariane could no longer make him suffer.

16. A SUPPER

THEY SUPPED together on New Year's Eve outside Moscow, at Jahr's. Ariane drank champagne and cheered up. Onstage a gypsy chorus sang strange melodies to a herky-jerky rhythm. Their nasal voices evoked a licentious and feverish Orient. At midnight Ariane offered her glass to Constantin and took that of her lover.

"Who will you dine with next year?" she asked. "Who will I dine with? Bah—let's drink up!"

She emptied the glass.

They remained in the spacious hall for a long time, amid the noise of the company, the fracas of the orchestra. Ariane, indifferent to all that was occurring around her, to the kisses exchanged, to the arms slipped around waists, recounted with infinite grace stories of her marvelous childhood and how she'd discovered the world.

Constantin listened, leaning towards her. When she finished, he said, "I would have loved to meet you then. Wise old women and men who presented no danger but were full of knowledge would have raised you far from it all for me. They would have taught you how to dance, how to sing, rhetoric, poetry... Like Esther, they would have macerated you in spices for three years. And when you'd become a well-rounded adolescent, they'd have led you in a procession to my bed."

Inimitably, she shrugged her left shoulder and said, "Do you think you'd have loved me if I were different from what I am? What would have been the advantage of your being my first? You'd have abandoned me quickly enough."

They left. The night was cold; all was frozen. They got into a sleigh and, sheltered behind the enormous coachman with his padded sheepskin coat, headed to Moscow at speed. Ariane huddled against Constantin.

"I think I'm a little drunk," she said. "Last year on this day I was in the provinces. We had a supper and, like today, I drank too much champagne. But you weren't there to keep an eye on me."

Constantin clenched his fists. Once again, he felt himself possessed by an unhealthy desire to learn what Ariane had to reveal to him. He leaned towards his mistress and said to her sweetly, "Champagne excuses many things. If your story is a funny one, tell it to me."

"No, I won't tell you a thing. You don't understand me. And you're horribly harsh with me."

Not exchanging another word, they reached the hotel. Once again, Constantin's nerves were raw.

He took Ariane on his lap while they drank their tea. He began to undress her, caressed her, joking and laughing. And then, returning to his idée fixe, he said, "Confess, little monster. You talk about yourself with incomparable art."

"There are moments," the girl said, "when I think I'm mad. Madness is not what people say it is, but a madman is certain there's a precise logic to what he says and does. We don't know the hidden reasons that motivate him. We only see his acts and declare them disordered. And yet they too obey a hidden logic, perhaps more perfect but in any case different, and which we can't judge."

"Oh, what a little philosopher," Constantin teased. But he felt like a victim waiting to be sacrificed by a high priest.

"It's certain," Ariane continued gravely, "that our logic is fragile. We normally act in a certain way. We think we're capable of this and not that. But one glass of champagne too many and suddenly we're transformed...We were dining, a group of young people, at the restaurant at the Hôtel de Londres on New Year's Eve. There were Gypsies, like this evening, wine, and that typically Russian atmosphere you don't know...and conversations more intoxicating than wine. It was after midnight...Handsome Dr. Vladimir Ivanovich entered the room. He came over to us, sat next to me, and, looking me straight in the eye, drank to the new year, which, he said, would bring him happiness. I understood what he was thinking of and, suddenly impelled by a secret force, responded, 'To the New Year!' At the very moment he spoke, I felt I'd surrender to a temptation I'd always fought off, but which now seemed irresistible. For two years Aunt Varvara had constantly praised the doctor in the long conversations we had together. He was a superman! He was unique among the eighteen lovers on her list. The others were prophets of this new messiah. The songs of praise to the handsome doctor she sang had ended up piquing my curiosity. I wasn't in love with him, but I often wondered what exceptional virtues Vladimir Ivanovich possessed. It's not wise to awaken the curiosity of a woman, and with this devil pushing her, what is she not capable of? I thought of the fable of Pandora's box...The doctor, as I've told you, was madly in love with me. If he hadn't paid any attention to me, perhaps I'd have tried to attract him. No, the only desire I felt was that of curiosity. I debated myself as to why I should refuse to carry out an experiment with Vladimir Ivanovich.

What was this man, whom my aunt declared was extraordinary, worth? What lesson would I learn from that incomparable lover? This was how I reasoned, but something held me back. It was as if I was cheating on you once, only once. You wouldn't know about it, so you wouldn't suffer from it. But there was something repugnant about sharing a lover with her... Anyway, I was quite pleasantly occupied elsewhere, so in short, I kept the doctor at a distance. And then, this evening, at supper, as he emptied his glass of champagne, every sentiment other than that of curiosity was abolished in me. I said to myself, 'How absurd I was. What was all that? Nothing; in truth, nothing. Don't I have the right to do what I want and to finally know this admirable secret?' I ask that you note that I was no more in love than I was in the past. I looked on Vladimir Ivanovich as I had the day before. But I obeyed the laws of a new logic before which everything bowed. I was unpleasant with him for the rest of the supper, even more so because he had an irritating air of self-assuredness. He listened to my insolent remarks with a half smile. I wanted to slap him. To make a long story short, he stole me from my knight and placed me in his sleigh. 'I'm going to the boulevard,' I said. 'All right, then, to the boulevard,' he said to the coachman, and we sped off in the frozen night, me half lying in his arms, as tradition dictates. I was numb, far from myself, and yet I preserved an extreme lucidity of mind. I looked at myself with great interest. I felt I was watching a performance. He didn't speak. The only thing he said was to the coachman when we'd driven several versts on the boulevard: 'Home,' he said. I listened without protesting. We reached his house. He has a small apartment where he receives his clients and which is separate from his home. We entered... How warm it was in the sitting room!

I spoke and the sound of my voice surprised me ... There was too much light ..."

Ariane stopped her tale here. Constantin thought she looked pale.

"But you're squeezing me. I can hardly breathe," she said, trying to pull herself free.

He saw that in fact his arm was squeezing her frail breast so tightly that he was suffocating her. He loosened his embrace. Silence fell.

"And then?" he asked.

"And then," she said, "what had to happen happened. And it was only then that Vladimir Ivanovich was as mediocre as the rest, except you, of course," she said with an ironic smile. "And that my aunt—"

At this point Constantin pushed her away so brutally that she fell to the parquet floor, her head striking the foot of the table. She remained crumpled on the ground, a small formless mass, heaving rhythmically with sobs.

Constantin took a few hesitant steps, then grabbed his coat and fur hat and left, slamming the door behind him.

He didn't return until six in the morning. Ariane was lying under a shawl on the sofa. She was sleeping.

"Come to bed," he said gruffly.

She pretended to resist. He pulled her roughly by the arm. Submissive, she went to the bedroom. They fell asleep alongside each other, not speaking. Only a few centimeters separated them, but it seemed like an unbridgeable abyss.

17. JUVENILIA

CONSTANTIN'S business detained him a few more weeks, during which he continued to live with Ariane. He didn't have the strength to break up and remain in Moscow. The day of the inevitable break he would have to leave the city and flee to Petersburg.

Knowing the girl's character and how central pride was in her upbringing, he realized all he had to do for her to immediately leave him was to determine to put an end to things. This proud girl would be capable, out of spite, of taking a lover the day of their breakup in order to render any return impossible. She wouldn't write, she wouldn't call, she wouldn't follow him to Petersburg.

At the same time that his determination to leave her grew stronger, he lived with her in an unchanged intimacy, but he looked on her as someone to whom he'd been closely attached and was about to lose. At the moment of breaking up with her, and when the sacrifice was already carried out in his mind, he spoke to her more sweetly. He didn't lose his self-control; he didn't treat her harshly. He no longer had that glacial dryness he'd employed as armor against her. They now had long conversations without any arguments. They both avoided dangerous subjects, irritating questions, words from which sparks fly.

He often had her tell stories of her passionate childhood.

One evening, in response to an inappropriate remark on her part, he laughingly told her, "You weren't brought up right, little one."

"That's not true," she responded. "I wasn't brought up at all. If it will amuse you, I'll tell you how I spent my childhood. When I was little we had an apartment for the winter in Rome. My mother was beautiful, elegant, courted. I lived separately with my governess, a Frenchwoman, Mlle Victoire. She was a spinster of forty, pious, good, unintelligent, submissive to all my whims. When I was a small child I was a little phenomenon; that is, I—my memory—was so retentive that I only had to read something once to know it by heart. And since no one worried about what I was up to, you can see what this might have led to. I'd learned to read almost on my own at age four. I remember that a chemistry book fell into my hands. I learned its first page, and one day, during a lunch attended by several people, my godfather asked me what I knew, at which point I recited my page of chemistry without skipping a word. It goes without saying that I didn't understand a thing, but they didn't know any more than I ... They were agog with admiration. Praise, compliments without end ... My mother, who never took care of me, was proud as punch. As a result, when later there was a gathering in the sitting room, I was called for. Mlle Victoire put a white dress with a beautiful sash on me, curled my hair, and I made my entry. I had to recount fables. And the women kissed me and the men questioned me. Nothing could have been more disagreeable than the kisses of these powdered women. When they took me in their arms I said, 'Quickly. Not on the lips, and don't slobber on me.' At which point all those fools laughed. I soon found it humiliating to be exhibited like a trained dog and refused to appear in the salon. Big scandal. My father came to get me. His entreaties, his threats, were in vain. I clung to my bed and, when he tried to take me, the house echoed with my cries. They ended up allowing me to live in peace with Mlle Victoire. We went on long walks together and I took her to the filthiest quarters of Rome. The poor girl was frightened, begged me to go back home, kept making the sign of the cross, and dragged me into the first church we saw. There she prayed in order to recover from the excitement, and lit a candle, while I amused myself on my own, hopping from one paving stone to another.

"Later, when I was ten or twelve, my mother put me to use. She had guessed that I had nothing but scorn for my father and that though there was no closeness between her and me, I would never betray her.

"Why did I feel this way about my father? I rarely saw him, for he was always traveling. I remember that when I was still very little, I felt that he didn't love me. He would always look at me strangely. He was very kind, but he treated me like a doll. When he spoke of me to my mother he always said, 'That little one ... That little one is very intelligent ... That little one is strange ...,' et cetera, et cetera. He never yelled at me, but he was like a stranger who lived with us a few months of the year. Once I witnessed a violent scene between him and my mother. He had arrived unexpectedly from Petersburg. What did he find at home that displeased him? I have no idea, but at table, after my mother said something, he became angry and, for what reason I don't know, showered her with criticism. She replied sharply. He then rose, threw his napkin down, and said, 'I'm leaving and never coming back.' 'Bon voyage,' my mother responded. He kissed me and left. At that moment I felt great respect for him. It seemed to me he'd acted like a hero. He left that very evening for Paris. Never had I thought so highly of my father. He hadn't surrendered. He had done what he'd resolved to do. I admired him for two weeks. And then suddenly one morning I found him in my mother's bedroom sitting on the bed. He had arrived during the night. When I went in I felt like I was disturbing him. They were laughing loudly together and my mother was playing with a pearl necklace he'd brought her. Since that day I've had nothing but contempt for him.

"But that's not what I wanted to talk about. I wanted to tell you how my mother used me for more obscure purposes, about which she told me nothing.

"I was already grown. We were in Cannes that winter and had a villa in La Californie. I went to class every morning in town, accompanied by Mlle Victoire, and came home alone on the tram, since I couldn't accept always being escorted by the good Victoire. Mama had gone along with this, which surprised me, giving me errands to run for her. I was proud of having earned my independence at twelve. One day my mother said to me, 'Go to the post office and ask if there's anything for this number.'

"She handed me a little piece of paper on which was written 'X.B. one sixty-seven poste restante.' After school I went to the post office and handed the slip to the clerk. The employee, an old man in glasses, looked at me, shrugged, muttered, 'This is really sad,' reached for a stack of letters, and, taking one out, threw it at me with ill humor. I brought it to Mama, who kissed me and gave me chocolate. The same ploy occurred at regular intervals. She never told me that I should hide my trips to the post office, but I felt there was a secret just between us. If my father was near her when I came home with a letter, I didn't hand it over. One spring day I went up to the window and my father suddenly appeared before me.

"'What are you doing here?' he asked in an affectionate tone.

"I was troubled for a moment. I immediately realized that he had been lying in wait for me and suspected what I was up to. But at the same time I understood he'd made a tactical error. Had he waited two more minutes, I would have been caught. I said to myself, 'What stupidity! It doesn't surprise me at all about him.'

"'I'm buying stamps.'

"'But we have them at home,' he said harshly.

"'For you and Mama, perhaps. I buy my own for my correspondence.'

"He wasn't able to drag anything out of me. I didn't say a word to Mama about the incident. How could I have spoken to her of it? There was no intimacy between us, only complicity."

She stopped, gulped her tea, lit a cigarette.

Constantin remained silent and sad. She looked at him and said, "You want another event that will help you understand my relations with my mother? We were in Rome, a year before her death. I was barely thirteen. I spoke and wrote Italian as well as I did Russian. One day, my mother came into my room. She seemed to be embarrassed. She held a letter out to me that she'd written in Italian.

"'Listen, little one,' she said. 'Here's a letter I'd like you to correct. We're writing a novel in Italian with a friend, an epistolary novel, but I'm not as good as you. You need to help me, but only for grammatical mistakes.'

"She left and I read the letter. It was a mad evocation of love, in which the heroine recalled the intoxication of former meetings and begged that another be granted. It was full of mistakes. I corrected it and returned it to my mother that evening without saying a word. She thanked me and spoke of other matters. Obviously, I wasn't fooled by her tale. I remembered a naval officer who had often come to our home and who'd vanished. This is how I was raised, *monsieur le critique*. I dare you to make any comments..."

Constantin sighed and said nothing.

18. THE ARBAT

DURING the course of the crisis he was going through, when he was feeling anxious and tormented, Constantin frequently visited his friend Natasha. He left the stormy atmosphere of the National Hotel and took refuge in a new world where everything was sweetness, calm, and kindness. He seemed not to be able to live without having at his side the smiling sadness of his friend. When he was with her, the imminent split with his mistress, a split whose heartbreak he feared, seemed easier.

He dined at her home several times and didn't hide it from Ariane. Ever since he'd decided to break up with her, his tone with Ariane was different: he spoke more detachedly and made no mystery of his frequent conversations with the young woman. Ariane listened to him with indifference.

"I'll take advantage of my freedom," she said, "to go to the Art Theater with a boyfriend."

In the evenings in the Arbat, seated alongside Natasha on the sofa, they chatted while, beside them on the table, the samovar gently murmured. Natasha often remained silent, observing Constantin Michel. Sometimes he arrived at her home with his face ravaged, nervous, exhausted, cynical. Other times he was smiling, amiable, in control of himself. She guessed that he was going through a drama to which she remained alien. They never spoke of Ariane; through a tacit pact she never came up in their conversation. But she continued to live in their thoughts.

In the course of these peaceful hours Constantin sometimes took his friend in his arms and posed his lips on her shoulder. She didn't resist; she abandoned herself to these dangerous caresses. In doing so they freely prolonged an ambiguous situation, one in which Constantin's hesitations and the young woman's timidity were equally satisfied.

So Constantin was greatly surprised when one evening Natasha asked him a direct question.

"Do you love Ariane Nicolaevna?"

It was only a few days after the supper at Jahr's and the story of the young girl's visit to Dr. Vladimir Ivanovich. Constantin was still upset by it.

He gave a start when the question was asked. It was as if the voice that had just spoken was an echo of his own conscience. He thought a moment and then, having decided, spoke with firmness.

"No, I don't love her... I lived with her; I'm attached to her, for she is an amazingly gifted girl, bright and passionate. But for certain reasons that I can't explain to you, for I'm not sure I understand them myself, she has set out, implacably and with an infernal art, to prevent love from being born between us. Perhaps she loves me, but she'd sooner die than let it be glimpsed. I could have loved her, but she didn't want it. And so I decided to leave her. Our separation is imminent, which is why I can't speak to you about it. She'll return to her life of adventures and experiences I can't call romantic, for there's never been a colder heart, a head more reasonable in its madness, served by more burning senses...

And I'll be free," he said, leaning toward Natasha. "My dear friend, ask no more of me today. I'm going to Petersburg. When I return, allow me to invite myself to your home for dinner."

19. THE SCHOOLGIRL

IT WAS early morning when he left Natasha's. He went from the Arbat to the hotel on foot. The conversation he'd had strengthened his determination to hasten his breakup with Ariane. Verbalizing the thoughts that ceaselessly haunted his mind had made him understand that he had to bring things to an end as quickly as possible. He brooded over his complaints about Ariane. How could he continue to live with a wicked, cynical girl who took pleasure in torturing him, in making him feel his insignificance, and for whom he was nothing but a number in an already lengthy series? And in this hateful task she was an extraordinary artist in letting fly venomous shafts. He grew increasingly angry as he walked, so much so that he ended up detesting Ariane, whose portrait he painted in the darkest tones.

The lights were on in the apartment; its first three rooms were vacant. He finally found Ariane in the bathroom, and she was so different from the image he'd conjured on the way home that he stopped in his tracks, stunned.

She had put on a shapeless schoolgirl's smock that reached her knees. Her loose hair reached her waist. She looked like a grown, precocious fourteen-year-old girl, with shining eyes and a mouth already made for kisses.

She threw herself around his neck and remained hanging from it like a child.

"You're so late," she said. "Come see. I developed the photos we took the other week. Look how handsome you are. You're the Grand Prince, the unique... Me, I'm horrible, as usual, a total mess, someone to be avoided. Only the picture of me lying on the couch is halfway successful."

She held out a photo that showed her in the pose of Goya's Maja, dressed in light silk pajamas. Her top was open to a bare chest, a round, perfectly modeled breast standing out.

Constantin leaned on the door, so stark was the contrast between the Ariane who had accompanied him from the Arbat and the expansive child who leapt onto his neck. He looked at the picture, then at the girl, and joyfully said, "I like you more as a schoolgirl than in a photo. It's true you look like a troublemaker, but you can see that the appropriate punishments can still be inflicted."

"Just try it," she cried. "No one has ever dared to touch me."

She ran to the sitting room. He followed her.

"You know, I haven't eaten. I'm dying of hunger. Order something to eat. I'll tell you stories of my schoolgirl days."

A short time later, as they were finishing eating, she shared her memories of her time at the gymnasium.

"We had a priest who taught us sacred history. He was a charming man between forty and fifty years old, with a big salt-and-pepper beard and oh-so-happy blue eyes. We all loved him and he loved us as well. I would amuse myself by asking him difficult questions. I was fourteen years old at the time, and I caused a big scandal in the class the day he told us the story of Adam and Eve. I said to him, 'Batiushka, explain something to me, please, that I don't understand. When the world began, there were only Adam and Eve, right? No one else?' 'No, my child...' 'And their sons were Cain and Abel, I know. But how then did the four of them have children? At that time, could sons marry their mothers, like how under the pharaohs daughters could marry their fathers?' The whole class started laughing and the *batiushka*, hearing this, caught the contagion, and instead of answering me, laughed along with us. Only the monitor didn't laugh; she went to get the directress. I had such an innocent air that they couldn't punish me, but from that day on we were forbidden to ask questions during sacred history lessons. 'The mysteries,' the directress said, with a serious tone, 'are mysteries, and cannot be explained.'

"The good *batiushka* wasn't mad at me, and we became close friends. He often waited for me in the hallway, caressed my cheek, or took me by the arm. I was flirtatious, making eyes at him. One day when there was a dance at the gymnasium, I ran into him in the corridor. 'So, Kuznetsova, you're going to dance this evening,' he said. 'Come along, *batiushka*,' I answered, 'and I'll open the ball with you.' 'I can't, my child,' he sighed. 'We're not going to the dance.' 'So you don't know how to dance. Do you want me to give you a lesson?' And I held out my hand. 'I once knew, but I've forgotten.' He took my hand and put his arm around my waist. 'And this horrible robe.' 'Oh, it's no longer than mine.' So I began to hum 'Troika' and the *batiushka* began to lightly spin me around in his arms. Since he was bending his knees, his robe swept the floor, raising dust. We heard a door opening and he stopped abruptly. 'What foolishness,' he said, as he fled, laughing. That charming man . . . He really loved me. The troubles began. He had a daughter a year older than I. She was a tall, lanky thing with a face like the goddess Discord. But she had a great body and showed herself off barely clad. She had lovers the way a man has mistresses, and she drank too much at suppers. She fell in love, believe it or not, with an old actor, and when he left the city she went with him. Everyone talked about it and the *batiushka*'s position became difficult. But the directress of the gymnasium, Mme Znamenskaya, defended him and kept him on ... I think he took to drink after that misfortune."

They spent a charming night together. Ariane brought to life for him scenes from her gymnasium days. He already knew most of the protagonists the minor players circled. He was amazed by the prodigious art with which Ariane made the friends of her youth real for him. Her fairy wand conjured a youthful world, one whose shadows lingered a few seconds after the magician fell silent, then faded away and returned to the night from which they'd been invoked.

Constantin said to Ariane, "The city in Russia I know best is the one I've never been to and where you spent your adolescence."

20. THE SPIRIT OF PERDITION

BUT ON other days it seemed as if a demon had seized hold of the young girl. She didn't make scenes the way women usually did. She didn't raise her voice. She never complained to Constantin about anything he'd done. Her way was far more subtle, consisting of innuendo and vague allusions, demands, silences, reticence, of leaving him to guess what she affected not to say. In so doing she cast unexpected light on her previous life and on the experiences into which she had been led by her curiosity and "the ardor of her temperament"—this was the expression she used to make Constantin understand that if we had senses, they had the right to develop at their ease, as intelligence does in beings with a brain, like sentimentality in anemic young girls. She often enjoyed speaking cynically about sexual relations. Freedom in love was one of her favorite themes.

"We can see," she said, "that it is men who created the world to their taste and advantage. They imposed the morality that was most convenient for them and, through tyranny and art, formed a universal public opinion to which, whatever we might do, we remain enslaved. I'm not a feminist in the modern sense of the word: dealing with the woman question in the field of politics seems to me to be foolishness. What's the advantage of having us elect deputies to the Duma? I think we'll have our true rights when the prejudices that bind us more tightly than written laws are destroyed. I've often thought about this. And I'm going to tell you where I see the real injustice in this question—"

"Understand me when I say that—" Constantin interrupted her.

"Don't mock me; you'll see where I'm headed. Don Juan is an eternal hero among men because he had a thousand and three women. He boasts of it, and his glory and prestige are based on this. But how would a woman who'd had a thousand and three lovers be judged? She'd be considered the lowest of the low. People would have nothing but contempt for her. If she was not a professional, her family would have her locked up in the madhouse as a hysteric. Well, this injustice is the worst injustice of them all and one I intend to fight. As long as this injustice survives, we won't be your equals. If we take a lover, we have to do so in secret. Men speak freely of the women they've had, and we're condemned to silence. Why? Aren't we as free as you? Don't we, like you, have the right to take pleasure wherever we find it? It's in the interest of men to have many mistresses and that these women remain faithful, so they praise seducers in art, poetry, and literature and put a mask of infamy on any woman who's had many lovers. This is the point where the fight must be fought. Women's morality must triumph, and that's what I'm working at . . ."

Constantin looked at the girl, who'd grown animated as she spoke. He felt worry creeping over him: the storm was beginning to brew. He was imprudent enough to contradict Ariane by blurting out: "It's a matter of knowing what we want. Do you want to be loved by your lovers? If so, I advise you not to speak to each of them of the pleasure you found in the arms of his predecessors."

"Why not?" Ariane said aggressively.

"Because, little girl, you'll disgust them and they'll leave you."

"And if I want to be loved above all and despite that? You know me, I think, and you know that, like you, I don't like things that come easy, and, like you, I don't fear danger. I don't want to owe my success to lies. Misleading men, persuading them we've never loved before them, that they pluck from our lips our first sigh of happiness...What a disgrace! Do you feel like you have to engage in such deception? Did you make declarations like that when we met? So why should I lower myself? I want to be loved in such a way that people accept everything about me and that I be taken as I am, with my past... And if they don't want it, well, then let them go their way. And I won't feel the least regret for those who do."

She tossed out that phrase like a challenge, looking Constantin square in the face, waiting for his response. He remained silent for a moment, and then said with indifference, "There's much sophistry in what you're telling me, and sophism horrifies me. I don't speculate about what will happen in three thousand years: I'm a man of my time and I live with my contemporaries. If some woman among them isn't able to make me happy, I leave her for another. That's easier than changing the course of the world."

Ariane blanched, scowled. "Man is only strong because we're weak. If we were to show our strength, roles would change. You haven't left me, and yet—"

"Ariane, I beg you, drop the subject."

"No," she said. "For once and for all, let's speak openly. There's something awful and unexplained that weighs on us. We have to see things clearly, never mind the consequences.

I've always tried to tell the truth and you've stopped me. Today we're going to the bitter end, whatever might happen."

Constantin rose, standing before Ariane, who looked at him with hatred.

"All right, then," Constantin said. "I challenge you to tell me how many lovers you've had."

The young girl hesitated a moment, and then, carried away by passion, she said, "You want to know? Then listen, and today I won't retreat. The first man who had me took me when I was sixteen. I didn't love him but I wanted to know what that love was that we hear so much about. I drove him out the next day; I couldn't stand the sight of him. The second one, him I thought I loved; I was wrong. He was a fool who cried at my knees. You know the third one, the little house in the suburbs. Before leaving for Moscow I consoled myself in the arms of a student who adored me. In Moscow I knew the actor at the Art Theater. On New Year's Day, as I already told you, my aunt's lover took me to his house. In the train that brought me back, an officer who'd loved me for two years, and had the dexterity to slip into my car, won me for a few hours. I never saw him again. And then I met you, the eighth. Your reign was longer than all the others put together. Admire your strength and take pleasure in your self-admiration . . . Now you know everything. If we continue to live together, you'll have nothing more to learn. Decide."

There was a long silence. Constantin lit a cigarette, sipped his tea, took a few steps, and in a cold, polite, annoyed voice, said, "I can see that I have to ask your pardon for having kept you so long. But I won't impede the course of your destiny any longer. The day after tomorrow I'll leave for Petersburg.

I'll spend a week there. I think this time will suffice for you to find among your friends the ninth lover, who'll prepare for the arrival of the tenth."

As he spoke he went over to the electric bell, which he pressed.

"Why are you ringing?" Ariane asked.

"You'll see," he answered.

A bellhop entered.

"Prepare a bed on the couch here," he said.

Ariane went into the bedroom. An hour later he passed through it to go to the bathroom. Ariane was lying down, her face to the wall. As he came back through the room to reach the sitting room, she stopped him.

"Constantin..." she said.

"What do you want?"

She turned her sad little tear-streaked face to him and, holding her arms out, said, "Forgive me, I shouldn't have spoken ... I don't know what moved me to do so ... I couldn't stand it any longer..."

He approached her.

"How can I be mad at you? You gave me so much, and I won't forget you. As for me, what am I? Am I wrong? Are you right? We were happy together, even so. And now it's over. Adieu, little girl..."

He took her in his arms and kissed her brow.

She moved closer to him and, smothering him in kisses, whispered, "Stay."

He tore himself from her and, kissing her one more time, said, "No, no, forgive me ... I can't."

And he fled.

21. THE SECRET

THE DAY after this scene they awoke exhausted, as if emerging from a violent bout of fever. Ariane was pale, silent. She moved noiselessly around the apartment. She was brushing her hair as Constantin prepared to leave. His hand was already on the doorknob.

"You're not going to bid me adieu?" she asked.

He approached the girl and mechanically applied his lips to her forehead.

"Are you going to have lunch with me?" she asked.

"No, I have business to take care of."

"But you'll dine?"

"I've been invited out."

"That's not possible," she said. "It's our final evening."

Her eyes filled with tears she didn't try to hide.

"All right," he said indifferently. "Where do you want to dine?"

"Here. I'm too ugly today. You made me cry. I'm not used to it..."

He left.

That afternoon, crossing the Marshals' Bridge, he saw Ariane Nicolaevna in the company of a medical student. He couldn't suppress his reaction. "My successor," he thought. He looked at him closely. He was a young man with a delicate, clean-shaven face, with blond hair, asymmetrical features, and an intelligent air. He spoke animatedly. "He'll last a week," Constantin thought. Ariane was magnificent, her pale cheeks pink in the cold, her eyes sparkling, with something carefree in her step that was unique to her and that exuded intense life. She didn't see Constantin, motionless on the sidewalk, whose gaze followed her for a long time. When the couple disappeared into the crowd at the corner of Nigliny Proezd, he shrugged and muttered, "Time to go."

He was at a business meeting and didn't have a free minute all afternoon. Even so, he found the time to call Natasha. He spoke with her for a while, and announced his departure for Petersburg and his imminent return. "Prepare dinner for me," he said. "We have to make a big day of this. I'll think of you on the banks of the Neva. Don't forget me." He returned to the hotel on foot that night. He was tired and feared the final hours with Ariane. He would have to fight again and didn't feel he had the strength. He opened the apartment door with the apprehensiveness of an animal tamer entering the cage of a young, untamed, and quivering panther.

Ariane Nicolaevna had dressed for dinner in the finest taste. She'd put on bright blue silk pajamas, cinched at the waist by a wide cerise belt. The soft jacket hung open on her bare chest. Her unbraided hair was tied at the neck by a ribbon the same blue as the pajamas, and from there fell freely to the curve of her waist. Behind her ear she'd tucked a blood-red rose, and she was wearing high-heeled dance shoes. She was in a joyful mood. Nothing had happened the previous day; nothing would happen tomorrow. It was a day like any other.

"Do you like me like this?" she asked, advancing toward him impertinently, bowing deeply.

Constantin looked at her with amazement. It was a new Ariane before him, a troubling and mischievous adolescent, an uncontrollable page who seemed to have come directly from a comedy by Shakespeare and whose arched lips were going to launch a hail of sparkling witticisms. He was delighted at the thought that this disguise would give their final evening an unexpected tone, and responded, "You're charming. I'm ordering caviar and champagne."

Ariane played her role to perfection. Her wit and joyfulness were dazzling. At one point she leaned toward Constantin and asked him, "Please tell me, Grand Prince, that later, when you've forgotten how wicked I am and you return here, you'll invite me for supper, won't you? You see, you'll meet many more women. They'll have a thousand qualities I don't have. They'll be good, submissive, tender, faithful—though deep down I'm faithful, since I've never cheated on you—and perhaps more beautiful than I. But listen closely to what I have to say: You'll be bored with them and you'll think of 'the little horror' who put you in a rage for almost a year in Moscow." And then she said, moving closer to him and speaking almost directly into his ear, "Do you think you'll forget my ardent youth ... Is that so easy to find?"

"You're right," Constantin said. "I couldn't forget you, for in you there is a saucy mix of the exquisite and the detestable, after which everyone else can only seem lacking in savor."

"And yet we must part," the young girl continued. "It would really be too ridiculous for people like you and me, who are made to have a thousand adventures, to live like a married couple. But listen, I have a great secret to confide in you before we part, something I can say to you alone in the world and that you can never repeat, for I'd die of shame. Swear!"

"I'll swear whatever you want," said Constantin, who at the moment of losing her felt again the passionate desire to penetrate more deeply the closed heart of the young girl.

"All right, I'll tell you tomorrow, on the train platform at three, as the train is leaving, when there'll no longer be any way of turning back... And if at the last minute I lack the courage to confess to you, I'll write to you. I promise."

Constantin tried in vain to get Ariane to speak then. He wasn't able to drag anything out of her but the solemn promise that he would finally know a secret she'd long been dying to tell him.

He tried to guess what the girl was going to reveal to him. Knowing Ariane, the adamantine hardness of her pride, he soon discovered a path that led him to the truth. The girl loved him, but she'd sooner die than let it be seen. She loved him, she'd always loved him: this was the secret she could reveal only at the moment of their separation.

The certainty that he had reached that moment filled him with a somber joy. "Ah," he thought, "I've carried off a victory. She fought with a smile on her lips, but she recognizes that she's been defeated. That untamable girl has found her master. And yet everything is over between us. She made love impossible." Constantin hated her at that moment...

They fell asleep in each other's arms.

22. A GRAY FEBRUARY DAY

THE NEXT day was a gray February day. They woke up late, Constantin first. Seeing that he was dressed—it was after eleven o'clock—Ariane decided to get out of bed.

She sat in a chair, her back turned to Constantin, who was at the other side of the room, contemplating the charming and frail silhouette of his mistress in a nightshirt standing out against the window, through which a pale yellowish light entered.

And suddenly, without looking at her lover, occupied as she was in examining a silk stocking in whose toe she found a hole, she said in a nonchalant tone, as if asking him to ring for the chambermaid, "What's the use of your being intelligent and superior to others? Did you really not know that I was a virgin when you first had me and that not a single man had ever touched me?"

These words fell in the silence of the room. It seemed to Constantin that his heart stopped beating, that the room was suddenly illuminated, became immense ... He thought he was going to faint. At the second the young girl spoke, he understood that he finally had the truth. The memory of their first night crossed his memory like a lightning bolt; he heard a humble, childish voice saying, "I'm not fighting." He recalled the resistance he had encountered. He saw again the bloodstains on the white sheets. They'd formed a kind of tiny bouquet of red berries. But he had no need of this material testimony. A higher truth imposed its evidence and drove out doubt, as light does the night.

Overwhelmed by the violence of the sensations assailing him, he staggered. He could neither speak nor look Ariane in the face. How could he bear the fire in her eyes? To hear her voice was beyond him. He needed solitude, fresh air, a long walk. It took an effort for him to straighten up; to take a few steps; to cross the room; to reach the door; to leave . . .

23. RAMBLES

HE AIMLESSLY wandered the city for a long time, his mind a blank. He walked slowly, hands in the pockets of his fur coat, captivated by the thousand spectacles of the street. At the Sadovaya he stopped for a few minutes, looking at a large cart horse that had fallen on the slippery snow and was struggling in vain to stand up.

The wind stung Constantin's face. He continued his walk.

At times he saw Ariane again, thin and nude in front of the window. He mechanically repeated the words she'd spoken in a dead voice. He didn't doubt the truth any more now than he had earlier There was no arguing the obvious. But she was like the burning bush from which God appeared to Moses. She blinded and burned him. He could bear neither the light nor the heat. For the moment he closed his eyes and fled frantically, like a night bird in the noonday sun.

He entered the Kremlin, went into the Uspensky Cathedral, looked with pleasure at the icons. He recognized in the face of one of the Byzantine virgins the long, arched eyebrows of Ariane. The smell of incense floated among the mosaic-covered walls. He was suffocating. He left.

On the terrace that overlooks the Moscow River, near the monument to Alexander II, he suddenly began to talk volubly to himself. "Ah," he said with savage glee, "how well I know you now, pale and sovereign little girl! Today I know what intoxication for domination led you from the rooms of the Znamensky Gymnasium to the bedrooms of the Hôtel de Londres and the house in the suburbs. Your gaze, whose force I knew, saw men's desire bend before it. But by what miracle did you vanquish yourself and overcome the thirst for caresses that was only quenched in my arms? And yet you lived in a blazing southern city. Around you couples came together and broke apart. Aunt Varvara sang into your ears songs of praise to her lover. You remain pure, little Ariane, who belonged only to me. The triumph of pride that has saved you and preserved you for my kisses! And then a day came, and there we were, standing before each other."

A flock of cawing crows passing directly over his head tore him briefly from his thoughts. He followed their flight above the white roofs of the city. The discordant band circled, then disappeared behind the palace and the convents. He returned to his soliloquy.

"From the moment she met me she felt she was lost. The earth she walked on as a conqueror trembled beneath her feet. That haughty and scornful girl saw she was going to fall into the arms of a man she'd only just met, who didn't love her, who took her like a toy, who cynically asked for a few hours of her life in order to pleasantly pass a few evenings of his Moscow exile. I left no room for any illusions. I spoke straightforwardly and with no hypocrisy. There's nothing more cynical than the bargain I proposed to her... And yet she didn't even dream of resisting. She had met her fate. How much she hated herself at that moment, how hard she fought herself! But she was defeated; she surrendered. At that supreme moment she finally understood that she had the choice of humiliating herself either before me or before herself. She didn't hesitate. She took the roughest road, but the one on which, at the end, she could live without shame in her own eyes... So this passerby will have in his arms an easy, frivolous girl who goes from man to man as it pleases her. She agreed to my treating her like a passenger to whom you offer your hospitality for a night before sending her on her way the next day. Yes, but at this price she flees. She preserved a back room to which she returns intact...What did the rest matter? What did her lover and his opinion of her matter? She lies, and what's amazing is that at the very instant she made her choice, she knew how to mislead me so artfully that the most obvious material facts couldn't make the scales fall from my eyes. Through the force of her genius she created in me a truth that nothing could make a dent in ... Even so, the poor child had a moment of weakness. She didn't remain a master of her voice in the moment I tortured her and tried to penetrate her. She stammered like the frightened little girl she was, 'But I'm not fighting.' And I didn't suspect the frightful drama playing out inside her. I was blind and deaf. It is only today that I see things clearly; it's only today that I hear your appeal, Ariane."

He gesticulated as he spoke on the terrace, swept by a cold wind. The few passersby stopped, looked at him, and then continued on their way. He suddenly calmed down and took out his watch. They were waiting for him in his office. "Let them wait!" he thought. He resumed his aimless walk.

From the sooty sky a few flakes of icy snow fell, which the wind carried off in a whirl.

He couldn't stop thinking of Ariane's lie. In a flash she had understood its necessity and had immediately risen to vertiginous heights. Seeing her perched so high, he felt the fear we have when we follow with our eyes an acrobat who, at the top of a circus tent, attempts a trick in which he could lose his life.

But what was a wonder was that she'd had the heroism to play this death-defying role for nearly a year of daily life. In almost a year of intimacy she had been able to perpetrate this lie and sustain it over the shifting course of days and nights. The better she loved him, the better she hid herself from him, finding in her pride the strength to continue an impossible battle with herself. She saw the harmful effect of her tactic on her lover. He treated her harshly; he made her cry. And perhaps he couldn't manage to love her, because of the hateful image of herself she impressed on him. She had put up with this idea; she had suffered these humiliations. But in anguish and tears, in secret, she had exulted. The more he degraded her, the more she grew.

In the meanwhile, in the ferocity of the struggle, she devoured herself. She loved. One doesn't make room for love: once it's born, it invades the entire being. It had leapt at pride's throat and tried to bring it down. Every episode of a ten-month-long struggle was written in blood, for she took her vengeance on Constantin for every defeat she suffered in the struggle against herself. He noted a dramatic progression whose recent phases he was able to retrace. There was the story of the little house in the suburbs, a story intolerable because of its dubiousness. Then there was the even more hateful one about the hour spent in the arms of the doctor, Varvara Petrovna's lover, and finally—finally—the complete list of those who had possessed her for one night, one week, or one month ... Now it was over. She was at the end of her rope; the superhuman pride that had supported her had collapsed. She could no longer lie. A more powerful sentiment carried her along. She was nothing but love. And so the simple confession, naked, without a gesture, without any intonation, a thousand times more poignant because of the level tone it was made in, was that of the truth.

Constantin remained overcome by this inconceivable duel. He judged the heroism of the little girl by the immeasurable grandeur of the love that had led her, that very morning, to give herself up to him.

Suddenly a new, disconcerting idea occurred to him. He caught himself shouting words that vibrated in the freezing air: "If only I'd known! Ariane, what did you do?"

He spoke these words so loudly that the sound of his voice frightened him. He went silent, overcome by the new flood of thoughts that rose in him ... He imagined Ariane sincere ever since the first day. How kindly he'd have treated her. How patiently he would have laid siege to that proud heart and that sealed body. What tenderness would have been born between them. He would have taken her in the end, but how he would have given himself! But because of Ariane's implacable will he had been forced to defend himself against her. He had fought with a kind of rage not to love her, not to grow attached to her.

"Oh," he said softly, "why did you mislead me? How can we go back? Too late, too late," he said with despair. "What never existed can't be revived."

He stopped, stifled by the bitterness within him. Suddenly he wondered why he didn't run to Ariane. She was there, not far from him, waiting in a hotel room.

An inexpressible pain stabbed his heart. He felt, without looking for the reasons, that it was impossible for him to see his mistress again. How should he look at her? What should he say to her? What tone should he assume with her?

Mixed with the passionate and contradictory passions

fighting within him was an intense rage at the young girl. And now that he saw Ariane as she really was, he hated her. What refinement in evil had given her the strength to torture him for so long? She had experienced a satanic joy in doing so. Cruel and insensitive, she had worked with all her might at her vengeance. The full measure of love and hate, a sublime combination in which honor and lies, loyalty and guile, were strangely mixed. How disgusting. How magnificent... But he was worn down. A year of daily torture had exhausted him. What joy did he now feel at knowing he'd had her as a virgin? He was nothing but suffering. He sees her again as she has always been towards him. The old wounds still bleed. He has only one thought: flee, be finally alone, forget this hell. Yes, leave for Petrograd this very evening... But first to the hotel to pick up the luggage... He'll arrive at the last minute... Perhaps, tired of waiting, she'll have left... In that case, leave a note, a note saying he's leaving and he'll probably return... But he'll never return...

He looked around him.

He was in front of the little house in the Arbat where Natasha lived. "It's not chance that brought me here," he thought.

The minute he entered his friend's house he knew what he was going to say to her. He was breaking up with her. Because he was leaving Ariane, he renounced Natasha. He saw this in his mind like an axiom that one poses and doesn't demonstrate. An hour later he left the house. Behind him, his friend cried on the couch where he'd left her.

A sudden change had come over him. He was calm. He thought of his trip, his affairs. He went to his office. There he thought that he had to know what had become of Ariane, that he'd speak with her on the phone. She could no longer make him suffer or make him happy. For the first time in a year he felt like a free man. But at the moment he was going to call, he retreated . . . Why not see her before leaving? Why not dine with her simply, as if with someone he'd once known and to whom he had become indifferent?

He called a servant and gave him a verbal message to transmit.

"You'll say exactly this—and note well my words: 'Constantin Michel greets you, Ariane Nicolaevna, and requests that you dine with him at eight. He is taking the ten o'clock train.'"

When the servant returned, Constantin questioned him curtly. "What was Ariane Nicolaevna doing? What did she answer?"

"Ariane Nicolaevna was on the phone. She was laughing as she spoke. She stopped, heard me out, answered, 'Fine,' and carried on her conversation."

An hour later Constantin arrived at the hotel. Even before entering he knew he wouldn't feel any emotion at seeing Ariane again. He greeted her in a natural tone, as if nothing had happened, but didn't kiss her. He made no effort either to speak or to remain silent. He was frozen and numb to the depths of his being. The young girl was neither happy nor sad, neither sentimental nor cynical. She helped him gather his papers and effects. When they ate they spoke in an even tone of this and that. She didn't ask him when he would return. The question of the apartment in the hotel wasn't discussed. After dinner, as he was closing his valises, she gave him sandwiches for the trip that she had prepared herself and wrapped in white paper knotted with a blue ribbon.

When the time came to leave, she dressed to accompany him to the station.

She settled him into his coupé, took a rose from her bodice, and placed it in a glass. They then went down to the platform, waiting for the departure signal.

Constantin put his arm under the girl's. He didn't speak. He was very tired and his mind was a blank. From time to time Ariane sneaked glances at him. Accustomed to reading her friend's features, she understood, from his paleness, from the wrinkles under his eyes, that he was going through a terrible crisis. But even so, wouldn't he have a word for her? Would he leave her alone like this in the night? Was he leaving, never to return? She remained quiet, not daring to ask a question. The minutes passed; fear gripped her heart. The tension between the two lovers reached its height. It seemed nothing could break the silence under which they buried themselves, and that the separation would render eternal.

The three bells rang, to which the locomotive whistle responded. Constantin embraced the girl without saying a word. Now he was standing on the first step of the car's stairway. The train started up laboriously. Ariane struggled not to faint. She raised her eyes to her lover. He saw them filling with tears... Suddenly, gripping the support bar with one hand, he leaned towards her, wound his other arm around the young girl, lifted her, pulled her to him, carried her to the coupé, closed the door, and collapsed with her onto the banquette.

"What are you doing?" she stammered. "You're mad!"

"Be quiet," he said. "I beg you... Be quiet!"

He devoured her with silent kisses.

Arkhangelsk, October 1918
Paris, March 1919

OTHER NEW YORK REVIEW CLASSICS

For a complete list of titles, visit www.nyrb.com.